I0593531

To my best friends, Chrisi and Ellise,
Since I met you both I have been constantly inspired,
supported, and encouraged.
I couldn't ask for better friends.

The Ebonwick Chronicles

THE LAUNDROMAT AND
THE FOUR ELEMENTS

THE LAUNDROMAT AND THE FOUR ELEMENTS

SHELBY RHODINA

Shelby Rhodina

The five elements, earth, air, fire, water and spirit, are the fundamental components of magic that allow magical practitioners to direct their intentions into the world. When one of these is unbalanced, there is an excess of the element which makes the magic go awry.

Contents

I

Prologue

Wait, is it four or five elements?

Stuffed in a drawer in the flat above The Velvet Mansion, the Green Grimoire quivered. Its pages rippled slightly, and if anyone had seen it, they would have seen some of the pages disappear, the binding creaking a little as they did. Some things, it seemed, were not ready to be read just yet. One of the title pages had changed too, and the beautifully written letters across the top spread out to disguise that a word had vanished.

The Elements: Earth, Air, Water, and Fire

2

The Catwalk of Shame

"Oh my gosh, what are you wearing?" I asked.

"What?" Robert asked.

We were getting ready for our date that night with Lillith and Darling, and we'd just come out of our rooms to show each other our intended outfits for the evening. Robert's first outfit choice was ridiculous, and the more I looked at him the more absurd it seemed. He had on a thin white shirt that he'd rolled up the sleeves and left most the buttons undone, so you could see some of his chest hair. Over this he had a patchwork vest made from leftover quilting squares, and the shorts he was wearing used to be jeans that he'd ripped above the knee and had some pretty noticeable paint splatters on the butt. On his head he'd wrapped a yellow cloth that might have been a scarf though I'd never seen it before. On his wrist was a wide leather cuff, with some ribbons he'd tied around it.

"Robert, you look like a hippie threw up on you." I spoke, "And I mean that in the most caring way possible."

"Oh," Robert said, looking down at his outfit. "Oh man yeah, that is not what I thought I'd put on." Then he looked over at me and frowned a little. "Nav, you might want to look in the mirror too." He added before heading back into his room.

I walked into the bathroom and looked at what I was wearing. We didn't have a big mirror, but it was enough for me to see what I'd been missing. I was wearing a white shirt with poufy sleeves and long skinny navy jeans. Over that I'd put on a blue knitted jumper, that I was only just realising it had a large leopard print on it. The pants even had a small bear keychain swinging off the layered chain that hung from the belt loops. I needed to change; nothing matched.

I rifled through my closet, trying to find something else to wear. Just anything that looked nice would have done. The problem was that I needed to find more than one piece of clothing that looked good, and then make them fit together. I tried to grab some things that were fancier this time.

"You ready?" Robert asked.

"Yeah okay," I said. I stepped out into the hallway with Robert again and looked at him.

He looked like a punk, and that was a very hard thing for Robert to do. He was wearing this grey sleeveless shirt that hung so low it was almost a dress. Under it he had these red and black striped trousers that flared at the bottom and completely covered his feet.

"What do you think?" Robert asked.

"Looks like you're going to a concert for Celtic Death," I said.

"So, too scary then?" He asked.

"Yeah," I said, "What about me?" I asked, holding out my arms so he could see the full outfit.

I had put on a black collared shirt instead, and some dark teal plaid skinny pants. A black studded belt hung from my waist, and a turquoise blazer that I'd once pinned a brooch showing a skeletal women's face on it.

"Too fancy, you look like you're going to a black-carpet thing."

"Right, okay," I mused, "You dress up, I'll dress down?"

"Alright." Robert nodded.

We must have tried on all of our clothes by the time we were finished, everything seemed to be 'not good enough' for our date. We both had piles of discarded outfits spilling out into the hallway between our two rooms. Eventually, once we'd pulled everything out of our wardrobes, we finally found outfits that we hoped would work. I was still waiting for Robert until it was almost time to go. I kept getting up to look at myself in the mirror and check that I still looked nice. I adjusted the collar of my denim jacket, wondering whether I should even wear it at all. I'd spent so much time on my hair that I couldn't look at it without seeing a small turquoise rabbit sitting on my head.

As I walked back to the living room, I could see Robert sitting on the sofa putting his shoes on. He was dressed like I'd never seen him before. He wore a burgundy collared shirt and some trousers that he'd had to roll up at the bottom. His long grey trench-coat was draped over the back of the sofa, and he was putting on a pair of gold boots with pointed toes.

"Wow," I said, making him look over at me.

"What?" he asked. He'd even put some of his hair up so it didn't hang in his face.

"Are we going to an awards night or something?" I asked

"Come on," Robert said, "this is important."

"I know," I said, my hands looking for something to fiddle with that wasn't my hair. "I'm just nervous. What if we're trying too hard?"

"Lillith and Darling already know we're weird," Robert said, "trying too hard on our first date isn't a problem we're going to have, because they already know us."

"That's true," I said, feeling a little better. "You don't think it'll be awkward because we're already friends?"

"Only if we treat them differently on the date." Robert said.

"How did you get so wise?" I smiled, shaking my head a little.

"It's the shoes I think," Robert said, standing up and grabbing his coat, "you ready to go pick the girls up?"

"Sure," I said, grabbing my keys from the dining table and following him out the door.

I shut the door behind us and was very glad the rain wasn't too hard tonight. I had to walk quickly to keep up with Robert, he was almost skipping towards the art shop as soon as I shut the door. When I looked over at the art shop I couldn't help smiling, though my heart was pounding so hard it was drowning out the patter of rain that I could see hitting the pavement. We were very excited about tonight, and the excitement was starting to overpower the nerves that had built up in my chest that afternoon.

"Where are we taking them again?"

"I found out that there's a new restaurant themed around fairy-tales," I said, "I thought it would be something different and nice for our date."

"Good idea," Robert nodded.

We walked together up the stairs to the door of the girls' flat. We both stood for a moment, catching our breath and gathering courage to knock. I raised my hand to knock and at that moment Darling opened the door. Robert and I jumped on the stairs.

"Oh!" Robert gasped.

I felt so panicked I wanted to run back down the stairs. I wanted Darling to shut the door and let me try knocking on the door again.

"Hey," Robert said. Darling smiled and scrunched her shoulders at us.

"Hi Robert, hi Nav," she smiled. "You can come in; Lillith is just finishing up."

We stepped in and stood rather stiffly in the girls' flat. Darling sat down on the sofa and started putting her shoes on. They had quite a big heel on them but when she stood up she was only just as tall as Robert. She already had her purple fluffy coat on that always made me think she had skinned a purple yeti.

"Darl'!" Lillith called from somewhere in the flat.

"Yeah?" Darling called back.

"I need your help with thi-,"

"Don't come out!" Darling snapped, running towards the hallway where Lillith's voice had gotten louder.

There was a moment of quiet that we realised Darling had told Lillith we were here because Lillith called out again. "Sorry! Hi boys."

"Hi Lillith," Robert and I called back.

There was some more quiet before Darling came back, this time with Lillith behind her. My eyes widened, looking at her hair and what she'd done with her makeup. Her curly hair that was usually kept in braids or a mess on top of her head was now out and styled in the neatest curls I'd ever seen. Her eyes were surrounded by a shimmery green and she had eyeliner under her eyes which just made the hazel in her pupils look like gold. I had already thought that whatever she wore tonight I was going to be in awe, but I still didn't expect to be speechless just looking at her. I didn't even know if I was allowed to say how nice she looked.

Robert chuckled quietly and nudged my shoulder. I loosened up a little, but I was more nervous than before now.

"My ladies," I said, trying to look confident, "may we escort you out to dinner now?"

They both grinned as Robert and I held out our elbows for them. Lillith grabbed her bag and almost skipped over to take my arm. She looked at me, still smiling.

"You boys really dressed up for us," She smiled.

"Well, uh," I stammered a moment. I didn't know why I'd forgotten that she might actually want to talk to me. Or that I might have to talk back. I tried again, "Well, we are on a date."

"That's true," Lillith smiled, "Though I didn't think we were meeting the Queen as well."

"Oh, come on," Darling nudged her, "Don't tease them, they look really nice."

"Don't we?" I asked Lillith, raising my eyebrows now because I really didn't know if we did or not. I thought we'd dressed nice, but I'd completely forgotten what I was wearing by now, I was so nervous. I looked down and shuffled my feet a little.

Lillith squeezed my arm with hers. "You do look nice," she said to me softly.

"Thanks," I smiled, feeling my face get a bit hot. I didn't really care if she could see me blushing, just remembering my name was a little difficult right now and I needed to stay focused. Darling and Robert followed us outside and Darling locked the door to their flat.

"Where are we going?" Darling asked as we started walking.

"Nav booked a new place," Robert smiled, "Not far from here."

3

The Date

It was as if, just as Robert said the words 'not far from here' that the sky had decided there wasn't enough rain tonight. Within seconds the rain was coming down harder and none of us had an umbrella with us. A pretty foolish move. When you lived in Ebonwick, always having an umbrella on you is taught before you learn to look both ways before crossing the street. We'd walked just too far to race back to the flats now, but we weren't far from the restaurant now either. We collectively decided to jog there to get inside quicker. I was in front, seeing as I was the only one who knew where we were going, then Lillith, Darling speed-walked behind her in her high heels, and Robert was trailing a little behind us with his coat collar mostly shielding his face from the rain.

We got there slightly soggy but seeing the glowing sign that said 'The Grimm Palace' was comforting for everyone. I was excited to show the girls this place, it combined Lillith's favourite fairy tales with Darling's love of the occasional grisly murder. When Robert caught up to us we went inside. Thankfully we'd all worn coats, otherwise I was sure we'd all have been soaked through. My face got a little hotter when I saw Lillith take her coat off and I saw her dress. Well, not so much the dress itself but how it looked on her. The dress was as green and sparkly as her eye makeup was, and even though her hair was getting its characteristic frizz back from the rain her makeup didn't seem to have smudged much. Darling too had a beautiful dress on, it was flowy, orange, purple and pink just like a sunset. The sleeves on her dress were split so they flowed whenever she moved her arms, and the skirt was higher in the front than the back so you could see the shiny gold stockings she was wearing. Her shoes were tall and bright yellow, and would have looked like business heels if not for the colour.

Lillith shook some of the water out of her hair and looked at us sheepishly. "I think Darling and I should clean up a little, can you guys get our table? We'll be right back." She smiled, pulling Darling away to the bathrooms.

"Darling looked even better after the rain," Robert said, almost whispering.

"Lillith too, more like themselves I think," I smiled, "What do you think of this place?"

"It looks like a kid's fairy-tale nightmare exploded in here," Robert smiled, "I love it."

I nodded, looking around the place. Each little booth had a different fairy-tale theme to it, with carved panels in the chairs, and the tables painted like an eye-spy game that you could look at for hours and still not find all the details from the story. The bar was being manned by a girl whose fringe was so thick and long you couldn't see her eyes, but she was juggling bottles like she was a blindfolded professional.

At that moment one of the waiters came up to us and smiled. "Do you have a reservation?" He asked.

"Yes," I smiled, "Nav Green, table for 4."

He checked his clipboard before motioning to his right. "The Red Riding Hood booth, just over there."

"Thank you!" Robert said, so cheerful that the waiter was taken aback.

"First date," I explained before we went to our booth and sat down. The menus were already at the booth, but we didn't want to look before the girls got back.

I smiled wide when I saw them walking back towards us. Lillith's perfect curls had been rained out, and she had put some of her hair up again like she normally did. I thought she looked even better now. I wasn't going to tell her that though. Darling stumbled a little on the way to the table, clearly the big shoes were not something she wore a lot. Robert was looking at her with a look I'd never seen on his face before. If I had to describe it, well, 'strawberries that multiply the more you eat them' was the only appropriate term I could think of. I wouldn't have been surprised if I was making the same face right now. They both sat down at the booth with us, Lillith and I on one side and Robert and Darling on the other.

"This place is amazing," Lillith smiled, looking at the panels on the chairs we were sitting on.

"Feels a bit like, if the Grimm's fairy-tales had a church," Darling added, looking up at the arched ceiling.

Robert and I laughed a little. I handed out the menus and I

wondered what to say. This was new territory for Robert and me. We didn't know what we were supposed to talk about on a date, and we really didn't want to mess this one up. This was Lillith and Darling, there was no room for error tonight. The sudden rainfall had put me on edge, just waiting for the next thing that could potentially ruin the date that needed to go perfectly. Robert and I looked at each other over our menus, nervous at what to pick for dinner. I wished we could communicate telepathically, I wanted to know how he was feeling about all this and discuss what we should say to them.

"What do you think you'll get?" Lillith asked, her menu on the table so her question could be to everyone.

"Everything sounds too good," Darling giggled, "I wish I had three stomachs so I could eat it all."

Robert made the face again; I almost expected those cartoon hearts to appear over his eyes.

"Actually," Robert said, "We could all get different things and share? So we can all try everything."

"Oh!" Darling smiled, "That's a great idea, do we want to do that?"

"Sounds good," Lillith replied. "Nav?"

"Yeah," I smiled, hoping I could remember some more words quick enough. "What does everyone want to try then?"

"The Wolf Burger for me please," Darling said.

"Oh, that does look nice," Robert said.

"What is it?" I asked.

"Lettuce, tomato, barbecue sauce, and a mince patty with red cheese in it," Robert said, "plus 'potato pebbles'."

"Ohhh," Lillith smiled, pointing at Darling, "Seven Little Kids?" She asked.

"Exactly," Darling smiled.

"Do I want to know that one?" I asked.

"Wolf eats seven goats, Mumma goat takes them back and replaces them with pebbles in wolf's stomach," Darling said, giving us the softest summary she could. She did like the more obscure creepy stories.

"Right," I nodded. "Lillith, what would you like?" I asked.

"Cinderella's Sunday Roast please," she smiled.

"Roast pumpkin, mozzarella, spinach and garlic prawns," Robert nodded, "that sounds good too. Have you two taken the best meals?"

"No," Darling giggled, "I think we picked based on the fairy-tale more than anything."

"And I do love pumpkin and mozzarella," Lillith smiled.

"That too," Darling said, pointing at Lillith to show her agreement.

"Right," I smiled, looking back down at the menu again and trying to find what I wanted. It was no use trying to pick by fairy-tale either, because I didn't know any. I was lucky enough to get the booth that I knew the story, let alone pick out a meal too. I read over each item and was about to read them again when Robert spoke.

"I think I'm going to get the Grail Ploughman's." Robert said. "I'll get the drinks too, does anyone have a preference?"

This had never come up before. We hadn't ever had proper alcoholic drinks with the girls. We didn't even know if they did drink them. I think the only thing Robert and I did know was that a date was not an appropriate time to get milk-shakes. Well, maybe if we were twelve it would be alright, but we were 21 and we needed to look like proper adults. I thought so anyway.

"Anything with coffee in it for me," Darling smiled.

"Lemony?" Lillith asked, "I'm not really particular but you can't go wrong with a citrus beverage."

"Just as I would have guessed," Robert smiled, using his most confident tone. "Nav?"

He answered himself before I spoke, so we said the same thing together. "Anything blue."

Robert chuckled and walked towards the bar, looking instantly friendly and calm about the situation. I still couldn't pick out what I wanted to eat.

"Nav, do you need help?" Lillith asked, gently pushing the menu down on the table. I hadn't realised until then that I'd basically been hiding behind it.

"Yes please," I said, "I don't even know what I don't want, let alone what I'd like."

Lillith giggled, tracing her finger down the page. Her nails were black, I wondered if she'd painted them for the date.

"What about this," she asked, "Three Pigs Hurricane?"

"What is it?" I asked.

"It's a fancy bowl of chips," Lillith smiled, "with cheese and chicken sprinkled over."

"That does sound good," I smiled at her. The waiter came over and took our orders before Robert came back over with the drinks. I frowned a little as he set them all down, confused at what he'd ordered. Well, shocked more than confused, because for once Robert's drink wasn't pink. He always had a strawberry flavoured drink, normally a milkshake, whenever we went out.

"Robert?" I asked, "What are you drinking?"

"Well, I didn't really choose," Robert said, "the bartender picked it for me."

"Oh, that's fun," Darling said, though she didn't look very enthusiastic. She looked a bit concerned too that Robert didn't have his signature strawberry milkshake on hand.

"So," Lillith said to break the awkward silence that had been building, "I'm guessing you guys haven't been on many dates huh?"

"What makes you say that?" I asked.

"Why, have we done something wrong?" Robert said.

"No no," Lillith giggled, "You haven't done anything wrong, it's just pretty obvious you're nervous."

"Okay yes," I said, "We haven't really dated before-,"

"At all," Robert added.

Darling giggled at that too. I shrugged and looked over at Lillith.

"But I don't think we've done too badly so far," I said, "And we learn fast."

"That's true," Robert said, taking a sip of his not-pink drink. As soon as he tasted it, he made a face, sticking his tongue out like a kid. "Oh man that's awful. I'm never getting a grown-up drink again."

"Don't worry, I'll get you one this time," Darling smiled, heading back up to the bar.

"So, what would you two normally do on a date then?" Robert asked Lillith.

"Well, Darling would know better than me," Lillith laughed, "She was quite popular before she became friends with me in school."

"She dated a lot?" Robert asked, looking nervous.

"She'd had one or two boyfriends," Lillith explained.

"What are we talking about?" Darling asked, bringing Robert over a strawberry milkshake. He drank some instantly and smiled.

"The world is right again now," he said, his hands reaching out in a grand gesture.

"Lillith was telling us about high school," I said.

""Ohhh," Darling giggled, "And did she tell you about the monster inspired outfits she used to wear?"

"No?" I smiled, watching Lillith look nervous for the first time tonight. "What about the monster outfits?"

"She used to come to school each week with outfits inspired by different monsters," Darling explained, "So one week she wore all these shimmery blue outfits with shell jewellery and fish scale leggings, and she looked like a mermaid, the next week she painted an eye on her forehead every day, what was that one?"

"A cyclops," Lillith smiled, "I was pretty proud of that week actually, I found all these clothes at the thrift store that had eyes on them, and I looked like some kind of funky biblical angel at school every day."

"Actually, my favourite one was when you did the Loch Ness monster," Darling said, "You wore some of the mermaid accessories but with monochrome grey clothes, so you looked like the old Nessie photos."

"Oh that was pretty cool," Lillith nodded. "My only regret was that I didn't take pictures of them all, sometimes it took me hours to get ready in the morning, so my outfits looked how I wanted them to."

"Wow," I said, realising my cheeks hurt from smiling. I'd gotten used to the sparkle in Lillith's eyes whenever she started to talk passionately about something, but I'd never heard this one and she was more excited than I'd seen before. She'd tried to look nervous when Darling mentioned it, but she definitely had fond memories of her high school years.

"So, what made you stop wearing the funky outfits?" Robert asked.

"Couple of things," Lillith said, still smiling, "Partly because I hated getting up early in the morning, partly because I became friends with Darling, and I was intimidated by how she always looked so nice."

"I taught you how to still have your inspired outfits without going full on every day," Darling corrected her, "that, and you started dressing like a witch permanently too. I think your fashion just evolved."

Darling and Lillith smiled at each other before Lillith looked at me again.

"So, what about you Nav?" Lillith asked.

"What about me?"

"How long have you lived in shades of blue?" Lillith asked, her eyes wide with curiosity.

"Oh, that's a good story," Robert smiled, "Tell 'em Nav." He put his elbows on the table to show how interested he was too.

I laughed a little as I shook my head. "Oh wow, let me think." I tried to remember a time when I didn't like blue, but I couldn't. I attempted to think back to when I started my exclusive blue phase, and my memories blurred a little.

"Well, I always liked blue, you know what kids are like

with their favourite colour," I said, "But I don't think I was really, you know, obsessed with it until-,"

"Until we were thirteen," Robert nodded, "I remember."

I laughed, "Alright then, I guess I was thirteen. I was going into high school and I wanted to make sure I was always true to myself, even though I didn't know who I was going to grow up to be. I told my parents I didn't mind what they got me for my birthday and Christmas that year, as long as it was blue. I'm pretty sure that was my same answer every year. Even when my mother made sculptures for around the house, if she wanted them to go in my room she'd make them blue so I couldn't complain."

"And my parents always got Nav some blue clothes too," Robert said, "They love giving people gifts, and Nav was easy to get stuff for."

"When I got paid for a few little jobs I'd head straight to the junk shop or the paint store and grab things I could paint up or dye blue for my room too."

"Covered the walls in blue picture frames," Robert nodded, "He wasn't allowed to paint the walls, but he would cover them with whatever blue thing he could find."

"And when I finished school, my hair was the last thing to go blue I guess," I smiled, "It's been like this since then."

"I can't imagine you without blue hair," Lillith smiled. "What colour is it underneath?"

"Suspiciously dark brown," Robert replied, his eyebrows dropping to somehow prove the 'suspiciousness' of my natural hair colour. "Like a poisonous chocolate colour."

"Wow, I didn't expect that," Lillith said, "I assumed it was blond or something."

"No way," I said, scrunching up my nose, "That would be awful."

"Isn't blond hair and blue eyes the most popular look?" Darling giggled, clearly teasing.

"If you're a doll maybe," Robert said, "But Nav hates how guys look with blond hair."

"I don't trust them is all," I said, "have you ever met a blond guy, or seen one in a movie, that didn't cheat on his girlfriend or have some corrupt secret business?"

Lillith and Darling both laughed before Darling frowned a moment and said, "Actually, you might have a point."

I nodded, agreeing with her.

"Well, I think we've covered personal style for the night," Robert smiled, making sure to change the conversation before the girls asked about his high school fashion, "So if you two weren't friends before, how did you become friends? You guys sound like you were completely different at school."

"We shared a love of history actually," Darling smiled, "we preferred different things about it, but we were the only two girls in our ancient history senior class, so we were always paired up."

"I liked the mythology and artistic aspects of history," Lillith said.

"Whereas I loved the old-world technology, and obviously I always loved a murder story. The ancient murderers were always more fascinating to me because we still don't quite know how some of them happened." Darling finished Lillith's thought.

"I introduced Darling to thrift shopping for clothes too," Lillith smiled.

"Though I taught Lillith how to find the best deals." Darling said.

"Of course, as soon as Darling was wearing clothes that cost less than three digits, she started to lose her popularity," Lillith began to explain.

"And Lillith taught me how to express myself when I knew people were judging me." Darling grinned, "I wouldn't be this open without her."

"And I definitely wouldn't be this social without Darling," Lillith laughed.

I laughed at that too, "You only hang out with Robert and me, I don't think that's exactly social."

"How do you know I don't have other friends?" Lillith challenged, "I could have heaps you don't know about."

"Well maybe we should meet them," I challenged, "I'd love some more friends."

"What, bored of us already?" Darling laughed.

"Nav, stop pretending," Robert smiled, "You know you bluff like a walrus. There's no way you have the charisma to make any more friends."

"I could," I said, trying to look serious though I was laughing too much, "Maybe if I – or I could – no you're right, I don't like people. I only like you three and that's enough friends."

"Good," Lillith smiled, leaning on my arm playfully. Her voice went a little quiet and she added, "I don't really like that many people either."

I guessed from the heat of my face that I was blushing very hard at that, and I fell silent for a while. My heart was racing again, and I didn't quite know what she meant, but my brain must have fainted at the words and I couldn't think of any-thing else for a while. Luckily I saw the waiter carrying our meals over, two plates balanced perfectly on each arm, and the subject changed instantly to the topic of what to eat first.

4

The Walk Home

The rest of the dinner went pretty smoothly after that. We talked about our jobs and Robert made a game where we told the girls about an antique in The Velvet Mansion; and they would create a story about what it was and who it used to belong to. Darling always came up with the best haunted stories, and Lillith managed to shift them to make them funny again. Dessert was good too, Lillith and I shared a caramel cheesecake, while Darling and Robert had a strawberry mousse, tart, thing.

By the time we had finished and wanted to walk home the rain had slowed to the slightest pitter patter. I was relieved knowing we didn't have to run home, though the girls had both said throughout the night that they hadn't minded getting wet on the way over to the restaurant. Robert and I helped the girls into their coats, and we stepped out of the restaurant door onto the footpath. The air was cold and the water that managed to drip down the collar of my coat made me shiver.

Lillith slowly grabbed my hand and intertwined her fingers with mine so that we were holding hands as we started to walk home. It was a few steps before I reminded myself I wasn't going to get far without breathing. I breathed in the chilly air and my breath came out in a plume of steam. I smiled at the sight, watching Lillith do the same.

"Funny how something like that still brings us a smile," she said to me. "Even though we're adults."

"Well, it's like you said to me ages ago," I said, "We can't help being fascinated by something that looks like magic."

Lillith giggled a little, bumping into me as we walked. "I guess that, even though scientifically we know why our breath creates smoke in the cold, there's always a moment before that thought that we just enjoy it as something magical we can do."

"That's a good way of putting it." I said, thinking a little about how I'd had those moments before I'd even met Lillith or read the Grimoire or even performed my first spell. "Even if we try to think logically all the time, our brains still make room for magic first."

"I'm glad it does," Lillith smiled, "I don't think we could find much joy in anything if we didn't have that."

I nodded, looking at some of the shops we were passing. I saw one that looked like a little cake shop, wrapped in pastel yellow and pink. I couldn't see the name of the shop on it anywhere, but something told me that I'd seen the place before somewhere else in town. Maybe it was a chain of cake shops I just hadn't remembered the name of.

"What is it?" Robert asked, looking in the same direction. I'd stopped walking just before we passed the cake shop, and Robert and Darling had almost run into us.

"That shop?" I asked before the front door of the cake shop opened and two girls walked out of it, locking it up for the night.

Lillith's hand tightened around mine, and I took a step back when I realised I recognised them. One had a mass of red curly hair that she'd pinned up in a vintage hairstyle I'd seen on some posters around The Velvet Mansion. The other was dressed in black from head to toe and looked completely out of place in front of the pastel-coloured cake shop. Robert and I had seen them on our first day working in The Velvet Mansion, and they'd shown up again when Lillith had first taken me to the Laundromat close by.

"We should go," Darling said behind me.

"Come on, I know another way home," Lillith said softly, pulling my hand a little back the way we'd come. I started to turn around, but the girls had seen us and were walking towards us now.

"We know you two," one of them said, her voice had the same effect on me as a dinner bell; catching my attention and occupying my mind completely. I looked back at them, and the redhead was smiling wide.

"You work at that antiques store, right?" she asked, tilting her head to one side.

"Yeah," I said before I could stop myself, "And you are?"

"Hope," she grinned, "I keep telling Amara we should go visit you sometime."

Amara nodded, glaring at me from under her black, pointed fringe.

"I don't think you'd like what they sell," Lillith said, her tone cutting the air in front of us.

I shook my head, my thoughts felt a little foggy for a moment. Lillith seemed to be frowning at the two strangers, and Hope had lost her grin as soon as Lillith had spoken.

"Well, maybe we'll see you sometime in the shop," Hope said, gesturing to the cake shop. "We have free samples almost every day, and they're always good."

"Alright," Robert smiled.

"Yeah," I said again.

Hope nodded before she looped arms with Amara and they walked across the road, letting us carry on back home. As soon as they had turned away from us I knew something felt wrong. My hand had loosened on Lillith's while we'd been talking to Hope; and now Lillith had let go of my hand and was walking again in the direction we'd been walking before. She wasn't really speeding away, but because I'd taken a moment to realise she was further ahead of us than I expected.

"Lillith?" I asked, speeding up to get close to her again. "What's wrong?"

"I told you not to talk to them," Lillith grumbled, "something about them always seems off."

"What do you mean?" I asked.

"Well, how come whenever you get in close proximity to them you get distracted?" Lillith snapped.

"I-," I didn't know if I had an answer to that. "I don't know."

"I know," Lillith said, "I've seen them around town a few times. They seem to have that effect on people."

"And you think that's dangerous?" I asked.

"I think they should be avoided," Lillith said, "If you don't talk to them, you have a better chance of not doing something stupid."

"What kind of stupid something?" Robert asked behind me.

"We have heard rumours that the people they follow around end up disappearing," Darling said, trying to explain how Lillith was reacting, "I think we'd prefer if you two didn't disappear too."

"We have seen them a few times since we moved in," I said, "we haven't disappeared yet."

"Though this is the first time they have spoken to us," Robert added. I could see in his face he wanted to help the situation by being as honest as he could.

"I'm sorry Lillith," I said.

"It's fine," Lillith said, trying to brush away the anger that had seemed to cross her face. "You and Robert are just really nice guys, I don't want anything to happen to you."

I reached out for her hand again and Lillith linked her fingers with mine after a moment.

"Did you and Darling want to come to ours and watch a movie?" I asked, talking louder so Robert and Darling could hear me too.

"Actually, we've got an early start tomorrow at the shop," Lillith said quickly, "We shouldn't stay out much later."

"Oh," I said, a little disappointed. "That's alright."

"Thank you though," Lillith said, giving me a small smile again. "It's been a good night."

"So," I murmured, feeling warm in the face as I said, "So we did okay for a first date?"

Lillith giggled, squeezing my hand. "You need a bit more practice with some aspects, but yeah, you guys did pretty good for your first time."

I smiled, my heart racing so fast I almost couldn't hear myself when I spoke, "Does that mean I can take you out again?"

"Yeah," Lillith smiled, "I'd like that very much."

My chest and stomach seemed to fill with butterflies, and I felt like I could probably fly home. I couldn't believe it. We were close to our shops now, and Robert and I walked the girls up the stairs to the door of their flat.

"Thanks for walking us home," Lillith smiled.

"No problem," I said, following the joke, "We don't live far away anyway."

Lillith giggled, and I was so caught up listening to her laugh that I didn't realise she was leaning in to kiss me until I felt her lips on my cheek. I stood still, my face feeling like it had lava running through it. She stepped back again, opening the door to their flat.

"Good night Nav," she smiled.

"Good night," I grinned.

Darling followed her inside and I looked at Robert. He looked like he had a similar expression that I had on my face, but his quickly turned into something smug.

"Nav, we just-,"

"Had a date." I grinned.

"Okay, okay," Robert giggled, "Be cool, let's just walk back home."

"Right," I began to giggle too, "We don't want to ruin it now."

We must have looked a little drunk walking down the

stairs and over to our flat. Neither of us quite remembered how to walk steadily, and I was sure that it was taking all of our energy just to walk away from the girl's apartment. I unlocked the front door and we walked in.

"Can we?" I asked.

"I think we have to," Robert replied.

Together we took off our coats and started dancing around in our living room, admittedly sprinkling some of the rain from our clothes onto the furniture. Robert had his fists in air and was waving his arms about. I had scrunched my arms up and was shaking my hips back and forth while my fists did little circles in front of my chest. Robert started to laugh, and I joined him quickly, letting him grab one of my hands and spin me around in excitement.

"I can't believe-," I smiled.

"It actually went well," Robert said.

"It did! And she even-,"

"We even got kissed by girls!" Robert shouted.

5

The Barista's Power of Perception

The next day Robert and I woke up early. We were still excited from our date the night before, and the feeling wasn't even ruined when I opened my eyes and remembered how many clothes we'd dirtied yesterday getting ready.

"Robert?" I called out from my bedroom. I always left the door open a little so that I had a bit of light coming into the room, and this meant that Robert could hear me too.

"Yeah?" He called back.

"I think we need to go to the Laundromat before we open the shop today," I said. I got out of bed and was starting to pile up all of the clothes I'd thrown on the floor last night.

"I was already putting stuff in a bag to take," Robert said. He walked into my room and started helping me put my clothes in the large laundry bag he was carrying. "Nav, we did take the girls out last night, didn't we?" He asked.

"Of course, we did," I said, "What makes you think we didn't?" I asked, suddenly less confident myself.

"Well, it was," Robert's eyes looked a little glassy as he thought about it. "Perfect. Too good to be really true."

"Well, if you're looking for real," I said, pointing him to the small mirror I'd hung from my wardrobe. "That's a real purple lipstick mark from Darling on your cheek."

Robert scrambled up to look at himself closely in the mirror, turning his face from side to side to look at the slightly faded purple mark on his cheek. He smiled with a kind of dopey look that I hadn't seen him make in a long time.

"Is it weird that I want it on my face forever?" He asked.

"Robert, we are the kings of weird," I said, "And while I agree with the sentiment, it does look a little like a bruise."

"Yeah, I know," Robert said, still looking at himself in the mirror. "Someone actually likes me Nav." His tone was softer now.

I walked forward and put my hand on his shoulder. "I know buddy," I smiled, "Lets just promise each other though, that we won't forget to do things without the girls too okay?"

"Yeah," Robert nodded, "We're still best friends, and I think our first 'only best friends' activity should be to do some laundry and get breakfast from Silvan's coffee shop."

I smiled, watching him pick up the full laundry bag and throw it over his shoulder. "You're a genius Robert." I said.

Robert nodded casually, "Please inform The Neverbourne Times of my accomplishments." He smirked.

The Neverbourne Times was Ebonwick's newspaper, printed on black paper with white letters, and was extraordinary in its ambition to print as many joyful news articles as possible. 'Negativity is the death of sanity' was their motto, and almost everyone in Ebonwick had been in the paper at some time or other.

I laughed knowing that if I did write to the paper about Robert's great idea, they'd probably write and print it without a second-thought, and I let him head towards the door while I put on the last pair of clothes I had that were clean. It wasn't much, only a pair of black shorts that had frayed edges, and a black shirt with a skeleton print that I'd once bleached and then dyed blue. I put on a pair of scruffy sneakers because they were the easiest to get on my feet, and followed Robert out of the flat. We walked to the Laundromat, talking about the date so we could make it feel more real in our heads.

"Hey, Nav," Robert asked while we walked, shifting the laundry bag to his other shoulder. "About the girls from the cake shop?"

"I don't know what happened either," I said quickly. I'd barely remembered that part until Robert had brought it up. "I guess we just, pretend we didn't see them?"

"I'm not really into girls like that," Robert said. He seemed to be talking just to reassure himself at this point.

"Neither am I," I nodded, "I guess, maybe it was the surprise they came out of the shop so late?"

"Maybe," Robert said, "Maybe Silvan would know about the weird cake shops."

"I'm not sure," I frowned a little, "Do you think he would?"

"Well, he seems to know lots about this part of town," Robert smiled, "And he had good points when I was trying to get you to try the spell."

"That's true," I said, "Maybe we should ask Silvan."

We kept walking and we finally got to the Laundromat. Robert and I sorted our clothes and stuffed them into the machines. I did really like coming here. I liked the rows of white machines that weren't new but instead were classic, and the feeling that anything could happen here. The place was like a blank page for any conversation or situation. You could come at any time of day or night, and it would feel slightly different, the possibilities shifting and changing depending on the lighting.

"Robert," I said, watching him pour laundry liquid into the machines, "What do you think is the weirdest thing that's happened in here?"

Robert smiled. "Maybe someone came in with clean clothes one time and then took dirty ones out of the machine?"

"Do you think people might steal clothes?"

"Not unless they saw a pricey coat go in a machine," Robert said, "Or if the person doesn't come back to collect them."

"Why wouldn't they collect them?" I asked. I was having fun hearing Robert's answers to this.

"Maybe they got sucked into the machine and disappeared," Robert said, "Or maybe they just got swept up by the coffee next door and decided to live there instead."

"Oh, speaking of coffee," I grinned.

"Mmm, strawberry milkshake," Robert smiled. "Should we go now or after our laundry is done?"

"Well, I'm going to go now," I said, "But I'd be grateful if you could come with me so I don't get bewitched by the coffee."

Robert waved his hands, looking vaguely like a soldier standing to attention. "Right you are Nav, lets get to it," he smiled.

"Lead on my friend," I laughed, watching Robert walk out with his knees high.

We stepped through the café doors together, and as soon as we breathed in the air we sighed happily. Silvan turned around from the coffee machine with a concerned look on his face.

"Please tell me I'm not in a musical." He said.

"Oh gosh no," I said as Robert started laughing. "We can't sing."

"Speak for yourself," Robert smiled, "I've been told I have a sombre tenor voice."

"You don't even know what those words mean," I said.

"True, but that is how Mammy used to call my Dad's singing, and I think I sound the same way."

"That's very true," I said, turning to Silvan. "Morning Silvan, can we have our usual order please?"

"Of course," Silvan smiled.

I paid for our drinks and we sat down in front of Silvan's coffee machine so we could talk to him more. He had become a good friend since we'd moved into The Velvet Mansion, though admittedly we'd never seen him away from the café.

"So," Silvan began as he started making my coffee, "You boys have had an eventful few days huh?"

"How did you know?" Robert asked, his eyes wide.

"No one enters this café like they're in a musical if they haven't had a good week," Silvan smiled.

"Do people do it often?" I asked.

"Oh yeah," Silvan nodded, "More often than you think. One lady actually did start singing once and I had to make her coffee quickly so she would stop."

"Wow," Robert said.

"Anyway," Silvan smiled, "Tell me why you guys are in such good moods, I need to know."

"Well," I said, drawing it out. "Hmm, where to start." Robert started giggling and Silvan's eyes grew wider behind his glasses.

"Oh my," Silvan smirked, "You guys went on a date."

"We did!" Robert said, sounding so excited that Silvan gave a chuckle. He gave us our drinks and made sure no one was waiting to order before he leaned on the counter to talk to us more.

"Let me guess, the guy with the pink milkshake likes the horror movie girl?" Silvan said.

"She's called Darling," Robert smiled, "She's so short, it's adorable."

Silvan nodded, "And you went out with Lillith?"

"Yeah, I did," I smiled, "Well, it was a double date really, but yes."

Silvan smiled, "You're lucky Nav, she's a fascinating being." He said.

"She is," I said, my face warming up again. "She makes me think about things I never knew I should think about."

"That's the best way," Silvan said, "If someone keeps your

brain open and curious, that's how you know you've found a good one."

"We must have found the best ones then," Robert smiled. "Have you got someone like that?" He asked. We had known Silvan had a partner for ages, but he'd never spoken about them much and we'd never met them before.

Silvan chuckled again, his voice deep and comforting. "Dylan is a wonder," He shrugged, "He's always making me look at things I take for granted. That's for another time though, I'm guessing the date went well?"

"We were nervous about messing it up the whole time," Robert said before I had time to answer.

"We almost did," I said, "Actually, we had something to ask you."

"What about?" One of Silvan's eyebrows raised in concern.

"You know that cake shop chain around town that doesn't have a name?" I asked.

"Baked in Fairyland?" Silvan asked.

"How do you know what it's called?" Robert asked.

"They tell you when you go into the shop," Silvan explained, "It's a sort of 'need to know' business strategy."

"Well, we passed by one of them, last night," I said.

"And these girls came out of it, we've seen them before around town-," Robert added.

"Always taking photos?" Silvan asked, his white eyebrows dropping a little.

"Yeah," I said, "They've been in the laundromat before, the first day I came in here."

Silvan nodded, "My advice? The cake shop is fine, they make nice things. But don't get too friendly with the staff.

Don't even tell them your name if you can help it. They're not so nice once they know you well enough."

"Lillith mentioned something like that," I said. "Wait, she told me they worked for an underground modelling agency before."

"You'd be surprised how many people have more than one job around here," Silvan nodded, "But the two girls I think you're talking about; you best try and avoid them."

"Why?" Robert asked.

"Firstly, you guys have found some great girls that really like you, and you don't want to be stupid now." Silvan said, giving us a comforting smile, "And secondly, I've seen those two stalking people before. They're not as friendly as they look."

Robert and I were agreeing with him after his first point, but after his second I felt my stomach churning a little. Silvan had to go to the counter to serve someone and there was an unsettling silence simmering in the air for a bit. It was only broken when Robert's straw made the loud gurgle that signaled he'd finished his drink.

"We need to keep going," I said after that, "Pick up our laundry and go open the shop."

"Yeah," Robert said, pushing the milkshake glass away. "Thanks Silvan," he smiled.

"Yeah, coffee was magnificent as always," I said.

We started walking out and I heard Silvan say one last word of warning.

"And don't take the free samples from those cake shops, they're not usually as edible as they look."

6

Keeping Secrets

After we walked back to the shop from Silvan's cafe, Robert asked me whether I'd seen anything strange since we'd done the Binding Spell from the Grimoire. Since we'd done the spell a few days ago, I could tell he had been excited to see *something* change because of it. I told him that I hadn't seen anything strange, but I couldn't help remembering something that made my heart beat a little faster. I'd been so excited for our double date with Lillith and Darling that I'd forgotten completely until now.

~ ~ ~

I'd gone down to the basement, the morning after we'd done the Binding Spell. I'd packed up all the items we'd used, and the only thing left had been the Grimoire. As I picked it up it opened in my hand, and at the top of the page I read;

The five elements, earth, air, fire, water and spirit, are the fundamental components of magic that allow magical practitioners to direct their intentions into the world. When one of these is unbalanced, there is an excess of the element which makes the magic go awry.

I gasped and shut the book. I couldn't move for a moment, my legs felt like they'd been filled with concrete while I wasn't paying attention. I looked down; I couldn't see any concrete, so I tried to wiggle my toes. My shoes felt tight, I hadn't noticed that before. They weren't full of concrete though and that was good. I glanced back up at the Grimoire and opened it again. I read the first two sentences. I read them over again. Then my eyes skimmed the rest of the words on the page, not focusing on them but I could definitely read them. My eyes widened as I realised what was going on. Before we did the Binding Spell, I hadn't been able to read the rest of the Grimoire. It had been in another language, what had Robert said it was? Latin?

Terra, aether, ignis, aqua. That's what Robert had heard me saying in my sleep a few weeks ago. I could read the words in English now, earth, air, fire, and water. I remembered a history teacher explaining how the early alchemists believed all science began with these four elements. When they combined these elements, they believed they could create anything.

I shut the book again, this time without making a sound. I had sort of slammed it shut before and I felt a bit guilty. Not that the book had feelings. Well, all I knew was it had appeared on my dining table without being touched, escaped out of a locked cabinet that I didn't have a key for, and created its own ring of salt to sit in while I'd hidden it under my bed. Now I thought about it, maybe it did have feelings. I didn't know what magical abilities grimoire's had, if they had any at all, let alone whether mine was special because it *could* do those things. It was something I definitely needed to ask Lillith about at some point.

Thinking about Lillith made me start smiling. Not normal smiling either, I had a big dopey grin on my face considering how my cheeks were already starting to hurt. I shook my head a little and thought about whether I should tell Robert about the Grimoire, that I could read it now. Though, I wasn't sure whether I wanted to tell him. Not right away anyway. He'd probably make a big deal about reading the whole book cover-to-cover and I didn't want to do that yet. I wanted to keep my new skill secret for a little while.

It wasn't that I didn't trust my best friend, I'd trust Robert with my life. It felt a little silly really, but we'd never kept secrets from each other, and having one that I could keep from him was pretty exciting. To be completely honest, we'd never kept secrets from each other before because we'd never had anything interesting happen to keep secret about. We hadn't yet found anything that had changed since the spell we'd done the night before either, and if reading the grimoire was the only event, then I shouldn't really keep that information from my friends. I wondered if this was the reason people were always sharing secrets. Having the secret was exhilarating, but it was also a burden.

"Nav?" I heard Robert calling through the trap door to the basement. I wasn't close to the opening, but I'd had my torch, so I hadn't realised.

"Yeah?" I called back, shutting the book so I could walk closer to the trap door.

"You dead?"

I let out a small laugh, "I could be." I tucked the book under my arm and started walking up the stairs out of the basement.

"Well, if you're a ghost," Robert paused before I heard him sigh. "If you're a ghost, you have to haunt this place, right?" His tone sounded like he really was talking to my ghost.

"Robert," I said just as my head popped up from the trap door, "I'm not dead, and even if I was, I'm not going anywhere."

"What makes you say that?"

My eyebrows furrowed as I realised that wasn't the first time I'd heard that phrase. I'd heard someone say those exact words, 'I'm not dead, and even if I was, I'm not going anywhere.' Though the only memory I had attached to the phrase was a very angry voice saying them, almost threatening whoever they were talking to.

"I don't know," I replied, "I seem to remember someone saying that before, when I was a kid, I think."

Robert raised a bushy eyebrow at me. "A memory you don't remember?" He offered.

I shook my head a little, watching dust fall in front of my eyes. "Must be," I said, "I don't remember who said it or when, but I remember hearing the words."

"Maybe you were a baby and didn't see it? So, you only have a hearing memory?" Robert suggested.

"Maybe," I mused. I came up completely out of the trap

door and tried dusting myself off. I could already feel the particles sitting in my nose and I fought the urge to sneeze.

"Gosh you're practically soaked through with it," Robert said, trying to help pat out the dust too. "Probably should get them washed, I don't think it'll come out otherwise."

I laughed, thinking about how people used to bang blackboard erasers together to get rid of the dust. Maybe if someone else got dust on them and we got thrown together? I was laughing too much to explain, and Robert's face kept getting more confused. I decided to let Robert share another memory instead and said, "Mrs Dovetan."

Robert started to chuckle along with me. "Do you remember how many pencils got stuck in her hair one day? She used a whole box and then gave us a lecture about stealing her stationary."

"Yeah, and then she started shaking her head out of disappointment and when they began to fall out her face practically went purple." I added. Mrs Dovetan was our third-grade teacher. She was lovely, but rather forgetful. She always had her fading ginger hair in a huge bun on her head, and all manner of objects would get lost in there. One day Robert and I even spotted a wooden train, though we had no idea how it had gotten there. I don't think we ever found out if she knew how much got stuck in her hair, but it was always a fun game of I Spy when we were bored in class.

"So did you find anything different when you were cleaning up?" Robert asked, "I haven't noticed anything magical up here."

He looked quite disheartened that he hadn't found

anything changed since we'd done the Binding Spell. In fairness I'd been a bit disappointed too until I'd found out I could read the Grimoire. I did wonder about forgetting my secret and telling Robert, but I wanted to see how long I could keep the secret because I'd never had the chance to find out before.

"No, I didn't find anything," I told Robert, "Though the spell said it can take days or weeks for anything to come back to us remember? I'm sure something will come up."

"How are you sure?"

"Well, we passed out after the spell, didn't we? Us and Darling. And all the candles went out when the basement has no windows or anything. I'm sure we wouldn't have lost consciousness if nothing magical had happened." I tried to sound reassuring, but I wasn't sure I'd quite mastered it in my tone yet. Robert was usually the one who did this kind of thing.

"Alright," he sighed, looking around The Velvet Mansion before looking at me again. My nose was starting to twitch from the dust, I was still covered in it. "You should go change and then we can do some more jobs around the shop." Robert said.

"Oh yeah," my arms raised when I looked down at my still grey dusty shirt. "I'll get changed and then we can, well-."

"Yeah, I have no clue what else we have to do either," Robert said. "We can sort it out when you're back."

"That's the allure of working in an antiques store I suppose," I smiled as I made my way to the staircase that led to our flat upstairs. "You never know what will happen next."

～ ～ ～

7

Speak of the Devil

The day after we'd spoken to Silvan, Lillith rang to tell me her and Darling wouldn't be able to see us for a few days. They had a big job to do at Gray and Hallward that meant they'd be working around the clock to sort it out. I was pretty disheartened that I wasn't going to see Lillith again for probably the rest of the week, but I wasn't as upset as Robert was. When I told him he looked like someone had eaten all his favourite food and there was none left in the whole world for him. To cheer him up I offered to get us lunch from the coffee shop on the corner of our street, The Last Drop.

When we walked into the shop Robert jumped at the glass cabinet that showed the cakes, muffins, and pastries made fresh that morning. I looked up at the menus on the wall behind the cash register and the coffee machine. I wasn't quite sure what I wanted, until Robert stepped aside, and I saw one of my favourite pastries in the cabinet. It was still steaming;

it must have just come out of the oven too. I waited in line, watching Robert's face scrunch as he tried to decide what he wanted for lunch. If he was still deciding by the time I was going to order, I'd just order him the strawberry shortcake. It wasn't a very healthy lunch, but I knew he'd be very happy to have cake for lunch. And we hadn't had cake for a meal in at least a fortnight.

"Nav," he walked back to me rather sheepishly, "Can I have a Kraken burger?" he asked.

"Sure, it looks good," I smiled.

"What are you getting?"

"My favourite," I said.

Robert nodded, "And a-,"

"Strawberry milkshake with real strawberries," I nodded, "I know."

"I'm not that predictable," He huffed, "I could have something different."

"What then?"

He looked up at the menus above the counter, then around at the little signs that showed off the special new items that hadn't yet been printed on the menus, before turning back to me in defeat. "Yeah, milkshake would be nice," he grumbled to me.

We stood quietly in line until it was my turn to order. Once the cashier gave us a number Robert bounced over to a table and left me to pay for our lunches. When I finished at the counter I turned around to see where Robert had ended up. I scanned the coffee shop, and my stomach dropped when my eyes fell on someone in one of the corner booths. I couldn't see their face, their back was turned and all I could see was the back of their head and shoulders. Glad they couldn't see me, I wished even more though that I hadn't seen them either.

Turning in the opposite direction I saw Robert waving at me, frowning a little in my direction. I walked quickly over to him and sat across from him.

"Robert," I whispered, "Jules is here."

"No way," Robert said, sitting up more in his chair and looking over my shoulder. "Where?"

"Corner booth, he's facing the wall." I said. I watched as Robert's eyes grew wide as he saw who I was referring to.

"Do you think he knows we're here?" he asked.

"Well, he's got his back to the counter, so he wouldn't have seen us," I said, "But if he heard our voices he still might know."

Robert slumped back into his chair and crossed his arms at me.

"What?"

"How do you want to do this?" He asked me.

I knew what he was referring to, of course I did. Jules had been a friend of ours years ago, but when we got to high-school we drifted apart. Well, I say drifted, it was more like how the Titanic just 'drifted' into an iceberg. My last encounter with Jules was rough, and I'd dreaded seeing him again ever since. He moved schools after that, which made it easier to avoid him, but Jules showing up so close to The Velvet Mansion now was making me anxious all over again.

"I guess we have to hope he doesn't see us," I said, my words slow as I tried to think of an idea that sounded less cowardly.

"And if he does," Robert said, arms still crossed and his eyebrows knitted together like a concerned dad, "we are going to be civil, and we'll see what he wants."

I nodded, "Yeah, that sounds good."

The waitress handed us our food and drinks then, and I was excited to get stuck into my spinach mozzarella pastry. It was shaped like a crescent moon, and was known in Ebonwick as the famous 'Flaked Moonlight'. Robert's Kraken sandwich was filled with stringy seaweed, huge pieces of calamari, lettuce, and halloumi cheese. He took a huge bite out of it and smiled, though I saw his eye twitch a little at the flavour.

"Strong flavours?" I asked.

He nodded at me, swallowing before he said, "Tastes just like the sea."

I laughed, and Robert looked back up behind my shoulder. Raising an eyebrow at him, he motioned his head to the counter behind me. I turned slightly so I could see out the corner of my eye. Jules had gotten up and asked the waitress for another takeaway coffee; black, three sugars.

"Thank you so much, have a delightful day." I heard him say, watching him smile widely at the waitress and barista before walking out of the coffee shop. I let out a breath I didn't realise I was holding, and turned back to Robert.

"See, no problem," Robert smiled as my shoulders dropped. I could feel my body instantly relaxing again now I knew Jules wasn't in the coffee shop anymore.

"What do you think he was doing in this part of town?" I asked.

"Well, ma' good pardner," Robert said, mimicking a Hollywood cowboy accent, "I'm sure there's enough space in this here town for the three of us, it don't mean he was expecting to bump into us at this here parlour."

"Wow," I said, "you are terrible at that."

Robert laughed, "I know, that's why I do it. Why do you care anyway? We're never going to know unless we ask him, and that's not going to happen, right?"

"Right," I nodded. "I guess it just feels strange, you know, after everything."

"Out of all the coffee shops in Ebonwick, he had to walk into ours," Robert said, his tone deep as he tried to be serious.

"Really?"

"Come on, you know you can't actually be mad at me." He smiled.

"I could try," I said, giving him a vaguely annoyed look.

"Nah," he grinned back.

After we finished our lunches and our drinks we were ready to head back to The Velvet Mansion. I was glad that it wasn't far, we were supposed to keep the antiques under strict supervision most of the time, and we needed to get back to do some cleaning. For some reason which Robert and I could not figure out, some of the antiques seemed to generate their own dust every day, and we had to clean the shop regularly when we didn't have customers.

8

And He Shall Appear

When we walked out of the coffee shop I felt the hair on my arms stand up and my stomach started churning again. Even though it had been about twenty minutes since Jules had left the coffee shop, he was still leaning against the outside wall, looking down at his coffee cup and stirring it steadily before he took another sip.

I saw Robert frown but he didn't do anything that made him look surprised. Jules looked up at us and smiled. It was a different kind of smile than he'd given to the staff in the coffee shop, this one had an air of familiarity about it that made me annoyed. We hadn't spoken in years, and he still smiled like he had whenever he'd come to my house for a sleepover.

"Nav, Robert, hi," He said, lifting off the wall as we passed him. I was glad the The Velvet Mansion was close, but I wished we didn't have to walk past Jules to get there. Robert turned to him as he walked towards us, but I kept walking towards The Velvet Mansion like I hadn't heard him.

"It's been a long time," Jules continued, oblivious to my attempt to ignore his existence.

"About six years," Robert said. He sounded just like he'd said in the coffee shop, 'civil and waiting for him to explain'.

"Yeah, uh, where did the time go?" Jules said, as if that was a normal response.

"Probably somewhere behind the fridge of fallout and the cupboard of high-school," Robert said.

"Oh, right," Jules said, still walking beside us towards The Velvet Mansion though he slowed down now.

"What do you want Jules?" I asked, stopping in my stride and turning around to face him.

"Well, I wanted to, uh, you see," He stammered, pulling at his pale grey sweater. His blonde curls blew around in the wind, constantly moving like his hair was alive. "I wanted to see what happened to us?"

"Seriously?" I asked, crossing my arms as I looked at him.

"Yeah," he said, trying to stop himself pulling his sweater by placing his hands behind his back. "I don't quite remember, exactly, why we stopped being friends?"

A laugh escaped my mouth, "Of course, why would you remember? It was hardly important was it?"

"Well, I knew it was bad I just didn't think-,"

"I don't think 'bad' is a strong enough word for it Jules," Robert said, stepping past Jules so he was next to me again.

"Well, that's what I came to find out," Jules said, stepping closer to us, "I've asked everyone but no one seems to know exactly what happened, they all just said to ask you guys directly."

"What do you mean 'they' told you?" I asked.

"Well, it was a few weeks ago," Jules said, "I woke up and I couldn't remember anything. I went and stayed at my mum's house a while, and I asked her why I couldn't remember anything since the start of high-school. Then I went to your parents house," He looked me in the eyes when he said that, "And they told me you were working in The Velvet Mansion, and to go talk to you."

"So, you've been tracking us down?" I asked. Of course my parents would tell Jules exactly where I was. They loved Jules, even treated him like their third son. They were devastated when Jules and I had stopped talking. I think if they'd had the choice they would have swapped me for Jules in an instant.

"Not tracking, really," Jules flapped, trying to make it sound more innocent than it was. "Just trying to figure out where all my memories have gone, that's all. I was hoping you guys could help me fill in the blanks."

"We still don't really know what happened," Robert said, "We had a falling out and then you moved schools pretty soon after."

"Surely you could tell me why though?" He said, his eyes searching us for answers. If I didn't know him I'd think he was truly desperate to make amends for what he did. Trouble was that I did know Jules, and this just made me more angry at him. "You could tell me how I changed?"

"Honestly Jules, we don't know *how* it happened," Robert

said, "We saw you less and less, and then suddenly you weren't someone we knew anymore. You just, changed."

"And after six years," I added, "we don't really want to know this new Jules either."

He looked surprised, then his face fell, and then it lifted again like he'd already accepted that this was how the conversation would end. "You know, that's okay," He said, his lips turning slightly into a polite smile, "I thought it might be a bad idea to come here, I mean, no one else could tell me anything so I guessed it wasn't going to be good."

"Yeah, you could say that," I said, turning around to keep walking towards The Velvet Mansion. I could feel Robert start to turn with me a little reluctantly. I started walking, looking both ways down the street before starting to cross. I heard Jules stop Robert before he could follow me. Once I got to the other side of the road I turned back, watching Robert pocket something before walking across the road after me.

I made eye contact with Jules, he gave us a small wave before turning around and walking back up the street past The Last Drop.

"What was that?" I asked Robert, walking with him towards the door of our apartment.

"He gave me his number, just in case we had a change of heart and wanted to talk about what happened," Robert explained, showing me a card with some roughly drawn numbers written on it.

"You should throw it out," I said.

He shrugged at me gently, "Might hold onto it, just in case something changes my mind."

"Do what you want," I said, my tone a little harsh. Though I wasn't going to stop him talking to Jules, I knew it would take something pretty impressive to convince me that Jules deserved a second chance. "So what do you say, tea?"

"Yes please," Robert said, following me into our apartment.

9

Lillith and Magic Secrets

Over the next week, Robert asked me a few times if I'd noticed anything different that might prove the Binding Spell had worked. I kept telling him I hadn't noticed anything special yet, though of course that was a lie. I had opened the Grimoire once or twice since I'd found I could read it, but all I'd managed to read was those first two sentences over and over again. It wasn't that I was worried about what I might read, more that I was worried the deeper I got into the book the more likely my parents would find out sooner or later. I still felt the familiar dread I did when I was living at home and wondered if I could learn even a little about magic without my parents finding out. I had wondered about it before, though if I ever thought about it I'd be told on by my little brother just hours later. It was the same now, opening the Grimoire and trying to read past those two sentences. Each time I got to the word 'awry' I stopped, the hair on the back of my neck tingled so much it was giving me a headache. I'd thought this would be easier now, since I'd already done a spell with Robert and the girls, but it seemed harder almost.

I had the book propped up on my knees as I sat scrunched up in my armchair. Robert had decided he was going to keep tinkering in the store for a while after we closed up, so I decided to try and read the Grimoire again. Even just an extra couple of words would be enough. I muttered the names of the elements under my breath; earth, air, water and fire. Something seemed to be different about reading them this time, like I was forgetting something. I was starting to get frustrated as my eyes kept going in and out of focus on the word 'elements'. Then I had to shut the book again and sit up straight. Maybe I just couldn't do it today; I didn't have the energy. I resigned to taking the book to my bedroom and putting it on my dresser before making myself a cup of tea.

The kettle had just finished boiling when I went to pour the water in my cup, but I heard a knock at the door and set the kettle down. I walked over to the door and wondered if Robert had forgotten The Velvet Mansion had stairs inside to the flat. When I opened the door I instantly started to smile. Lillith was standing outside the door, bundled up in a huge puffy green coat, with her grey knitted scarf over her head. It was surprisingly windy today, and the rain made it feel as if it were winter already. I could tell she was smiling even though her scarf was tucked just under her nose.

"Long time no see, have you got enough layers on then?" I laughed as she waddled in and made her way instantly to the coat stand.

"Almost," she said, taking off another coat underneath the puffy one she had. She kept her scarf on her head but she loosened it so it hung around her shoulders. "I didn't know if it was going to get colder or not."

"You only live next door," I teased her.

"Yes Nav, but I live *next door*," Lillith said, clearly joking too, "It's so far away when it's cold."

"Right, right," I smiled, "can't have a frozen block of Lillith in the alleyway."

"No, you can't," she said, taking a seat on the couch, "I'd be far too salty."

I laughed at that and then remembered I still hadn't made my tea. I walked over to the kitchen again and picked out another mug before asking Lillith if she wanted tea too. I didn't really need to ask, she'd never said no to tea before, and she didn't this time. She was sitting quite comfortably on the couch when I brought over our tea, and when I sat down I asked her why she was visiting. It wasn't as if I wasn't very excited to see her again after our date, but she had a strange look in her eyes like she was desperate to tell me something.

"Well," she said, taking a sip of tea. She hummed for moment before speaking again. "I wanted to ask if you'd noticed anything strange. After the Binding Spell I mean."

I was so used to hearing the question I started to give my default response I'd said to Robert the last few days. "No, I'm afraid I-." I stopped myself before I continued. "Really, the only weird thing was we saw an old friend of ours."

"Really?" Lillith said, "I didn't think you two had any other friends."

"Ha ha," I said with as little emotion as I possibly could. Lillith started to giggle at me. "The truth is he hasn't been a friend of ours for 6 years, so you're right." I admitted.

"I knew it," Lillith whispered cheekily.

"Honestly," I said after a moment of thinking about it, "I don't know enough about magic to know if something is affected by it or not. I probably wouldn't notice anything because it would just seem to be 'weirdness as usual'."

Lillith smiled at me, "Well, maybe that just means you need to do some more magic so you can see it more?"

"Maybe?" I said, feeling guilty again that I hadn't read more of the Grimoire. It occurred to me that being able to read it was definitely an effect of the magic. "Lillith, what do you know about magical elements?" I asked.

Lillith looked excited for a moment, then started thinking hard. I hadn't seen her struggle this much to answer a question before, the faces she was making concerned me a little. "I know there are four, earth, air, fire, and water. And that, in magic, they're the most crucial part to have if you're going to achieve anything."

I started to nod, "We had representations of them when we did the Binding Spell."

"Exactly," Lillith smiled, "Though I think there are some spells you can do without all four."

"Really?" I asked. I remembered the Grimoire's warning and wondered if Lillith knew about it too. "Are you sure there's only four? I mean, magic seems a little more complex than that."

"I think so," she mused, "Though I've never actually done

any spells by myself, so I don't know if there would be any differences if you missed out on one of the elements."

"Alright," I said, feeling a little confused again. If I could just start reading the Grimoire I could find out.

We sat in silence for a bit and drank our tea, which wasn't very hot anymore. I wondered if I should tell Lillith about the Grimoire, but before I could she jumped.

"Oh! I remembered something," she got up and started rifling through the pockets of her coats. "I found something that I think was affected by the Binding Spell, it's what I came over to show you."

"What was it?" I asked, feeling hopeful. I sat up more in my chair and waited for Lillith to find whatever she was looking for. Lillith kept looking through all the pockets, her tongue sticking out a bit the more she looked.

"This," She said, finding the thing she'd been looking for.

She walked back over to me and showed me a small box. It was about as big as her palm and covered in purple velvet that had been worn away on the corners. It looked like some of the very old jewellery boxes we had in The Velvet Mansion, though I'd never seen a purple one before. Then she opened the box and showed me what was inside. It looked like a medal, a brooch piece at the top and a frayed piece of ribbon hanging off of it. The brooch was an old broomstick, with what looked like a wand attached to it, and a large, pointed hat with a buckle around it. The ribbon was also purple, with a black pointed stripe, a light brown stripe, and a gold embroidered line running through the ribbon.

"What is it?" I asked. "It looks like a war medal, but there hasn't been a war in Ebonwick since before the town was built. And they wouldn't have had war medals then either."

"That's because it's not a war medal," Lillith said, "It's a medal from a coven. You would wear it to show you belonged to the coven, without normal people finding out."

"What's a coven?" I asked.

"A group of witches who do spells together," Lillith explained.

"Hey, that's us," I smiled at her. "Are you sure that's what this is? It looks way too obvious a sign that someone was a witch."

"In public most of them only wore the ribbon," Lillith said, "and they only wore the brooch piece when they were having a coven meeting together."

"Right," I said, starting to understand. "How do you know all this?"

"This is how I know it's a sign the magic worked," Lillith said, "My great-grandmother was a part of this coven, and I heard stories from her about it until I was around 6 years old. After she died, my grandmother took some of her most prized witchcraft possessions and buried them with her. But she couldn't find this brooch, and we all helped her look for it for about three months. We couldn't find it anywhere and we assumed it was lost for good, or that my great-grandmother had given it back to the coven just before she died."

"So, how'd you find it?" I asked.

"I woke up this morning and it was on my bedside table," Lillith said, "open so I could see it in the box."

"So," I thought for a moment to try and be as polite as I

could be, "How do you know Darling didn't find another one somewhere and gifted it to you?"

"Well for a start, Darling doesn't know what they're supposed to look like, the ribbons are specific to the coven and they're not something that just gets thrown out. The other reason is because I know where that rip came from."

I looked at the medal again, noticing this time there was a thin rip in the ribbon. I frowned, then looked back up at Lillith. "How'd the rip happen? If they're so well protected?"

Lillith's face seemed to go pink at the memory. "Well, I was trying to make one for myself, because I wanted to look as much like my great-grandmother as I could. And I didn't have any ribbon that looked like the ribbon on the medal, so the only thing I could think to do was cut a tiny piece off the original."

"So that's why it's such a delicate rip," I said, "Because you tried to cut it."

"My mother saw me just in time and gave it back to my great-grandmother. I didn't get in trouble, but I definitely wasn't allowed to touch it again."

"How old were you?"

"I was four. I was always surprised that she never sewed the rip together."

"Maybe it reminded her of you, just like the medal reminds you of her?" I asked.

Lillith smiled at me, "That's a nice way of putting it, thanks Nav."

I smiled too, my cheeks feeling hot as soon as she said my name. "So, you come from a family of witches then?"

Lillith shrugged, "Mostly just my great-grandmother, and my grandmother. My mother stopped doing any witchcraft when they both passed away."

"That's still better than the rest of us," I said, "you're practically an expert compared to me."

"Said the guy who did a spell and returned a family heirloom to me," Lillith teased.

"Yeah well," I sighed, pretending to be unimpressed, "We can't all have natural talent."

Lillith started laughing and poked me in the ribs to try and seem annoyed. I started laughing with her, putting a hand on my ribs to protect them from another poke.

10

Covens and Chocolate Pancakes

After Lillith left, Robert came upstairs and started cooking dinner while I peeled some boiled eggs. He still didn't really trust my cooking for some reason, but he had started trusting me with the smaller jobs. I'd told him about Lillith's medal she found, and he had been thrilled that the magic had seemingly started to work. Robert had wanted to go next door and see the medal for himself, but a deep growl in his stomach had stopped him. I thought he was cooking a curry, but when he put tomatoes in and started making mashed potatoes, I wasn't so confident anymore.

"Robert," I said, speaking over the sound of the bubbling pot on the stove.

"Yeah?"

"Did you know there were covens of witches in Ebonwick?"

Robert thought for a moment, stirring the pot carefully. "I didn't know about the covens," he said, "But I think I met a witch once."

"Really?!" I asked.

"Well, I can't be sure," Robert started, "I mean, it was a very long time ago."

I shrugged, "I've never met a witch, so I'm sure I'll believe anything."

"All I remember is she was a friend of Mammy's, an old friend from school, I think. And she came to visit us for a while when Christopher and I were little."

"That doesn't sound too weird."

"It didn't to me either," Robert said, "But I remember all the clothes she wore were black and the only colour on her was a ribbon she had on all the time. I asked her what it was once, and she told me it was a group that she was in. I remember I wanted a group like that, like a secret club really. I even asked Mammy if she could get me a ribbon like the one I'd seen, but I couldn't remember the colours of it."

"So that's why you wanted to see the medal," I nodded.

"Exactly," Robert smiled, "I wondered whether her ribbon was the same one, or a different one."

I nodded, thinking about the idea that there could be groups of witches in Ebonwick, doing all sorts of witchcraft together. I frowned a little and was almost too nervous to say my next thought.

"Do you think you'd want to be in a coven? You know, if we end up with proper magic one day?" I asked.

Robert laughed a little, "Are you kidding? We're already in one."

"Do you think so?"

"Well, a coven is a group of witches right? That do spells together?" Robert asked, "Well, we did a spell together, us and the girls. And we're a group." He added, giving me a smile.

I laughed a little, "I don't think doing one spell counts Robert."

"Well, I'm counting it," He said, "It's our first one, probably wasn't perfect, but it also took a lot to do it, and I'd say the energy would have been three spells worth easily."

"Alright Robert," I smiled. I'd finished up shelling the boiled eggs and I went to clear away the shells.

"Oh, Darling told me Lillith wanted the eggshells, I don't know why," Robert said before I could put them in the bin. Instead, I grabbed a glass jar we had just washed up and put the eggshells in there instead. I'd give it to Lillith the next time I saw her, and I smiled more at the thought.

"Robert? What are you cooking?" I asked finally, my confusion finally getting the better of me.

"Honestly," Robert said, turning back to stir the pot again, "It's a recipe Mammy used to make, but I have no idea if I've made it properly."

"Why not?"

"She never wrote it down and she always changes it depending on what we had in the kitchen." Robert explained, "so this could be right, or it could be something completely new."

"So a classic Bard recipe then?" I said.

"Pretty much," Robert smiled, "if it flops, I'll make chocolate-chip cookies to make it up to you."

"No complaints here," I said. I frowned a little before I spoke again. "Robert? Do you get bored of cooking?"

"Not really," Robert said, "I mean, it reminds me of home, the smells and things, so I don't get bored when I can make those things myself. Why?"

I tugged my hair a little even though I was trying to sound unbothered by it, "Well, you always seem to cook, and I don't, and I don't want to make you feel I'm forcing you to cook all the time."

Robert laughed a little at my response. "Four words my friend, Mrs. Green's Turnip Lasagna."

"Oh yeah that was awful," my stomach flopped at the memory. My mother was many things, but a good cook was not anywhere near being one of them. She always had ideas of fancy food, and none of them had ever worked out. We normally ended up eating toasted sandwiches my dad made. Robert's mother, Mammy, used to say that that's why I was so skinny, because of my mother's inedible cooking.

"Exactly," Robert nodded, "No way am I going to make you feel guilty for not cooking when I know your family's track record."

"Fair enough," I smiled. "Well, if there's anything you want me to try cooking one day you let me know."

"Actually, can you put the kettle on?" Robert asked, "I haven't had tea in hours."

"Sure," I smiled, getting out everything to make the tea. "I meant actual food though."

"Oh I know," Robert smiled, "when I come up with something you can't possibly get wrong I'll let you know."

I elbowed his side for his teasing, though I was already in

agreement with him. A faint memory did come to the front of my mind that I wanted to tell him though.

"What about chocolate pancakes? Like I made at your house once." I offered, "I could make them for breakfast, and we could invite the girls around."

"Well, if you're confident you wanna send your cooking out to the public," Robert said, "Yeah, I suppose there's little you can mess up with chocolate pancakes."

"Thanks Robert," I said, taking my tea back to the table just as Robert was dishing up dinner. We decided to call it 'Gumbo Surprise' because we had no clue what it was and no idea what gumbo was either, but it did taste delicious in the end, especially with the mashed potato. The only really tricky thing was boxing the leftovers up and fitting them in the fridge. Robert had made far too much, as he did with all his cooking, and we had to freeze most of it because it didn't fit in the main fridge.

"At least I wouldn't go hungry if you suddenly disappeared and couldn't cook," I said.

"That's assuming you know how to defrost things though," Robert smirked.

"Oh, come on," I rolled my eyes. I started to fill the sink so I could do the dishes.

"Don't worry," Robert called as he walked down the hallway to shower, "I'll leave you notes with the microwave times."

11

Baba Yaga Started It

The chocolate pancakes were a success! Thank goodness I'd done them correctly, I don't think Robert would have let me try and cook ever again if they hadn't. Darling and Lillith had a day off now they'd restocked the store on time, so they were very happy to come over to our place and have breakfast with us. Afterwards, Robert and I were putting everything away while Lillith was looking around our flat. We'd finally unpacked all the boxes we'd brought with us, and the flat had new little decorations everywhere. I wasn't surprised she wanted to look at everything, it had been a few days of serious thinking to figure out how to combine my things and Robert's.

"Hey Nav?" Lillith asked.

"Yeah?"

"What's Baba Yaga's house doing in your flat?" She asked.

"What?" I asked, turning around to look at what she was referring to.

She was pointing at a curious object that Robert and I had made in highschool together. It was a cottage looking house, that stood on a pair of chicken legs and looked like it should have been terrorising a small village. Robert and I had created it for an art assignment, but we found that we both really enjoyed making miniature buildings like it, and we'd made about a dozen since. I drew up the design and made the tiny details because my fingers could get into all the tight spots, and Robert knew how to construct the frames and fit little lights in the buildings to make them look real. We had gotten really good at making little houses, but we hadn't made one since we'd moved into The Velvet Mansion. Too much other excitement, I guess.

"Oh that, that's a project from school. It was the best mark I ever got." I grinned.

"Well, it is awesome," Lillith said, "But why Baba Yaga's house?"

"Well," I thought about it a moment, because I'd mostly forgotten what the house was meant to be. "I think Robert had the idea from reading some Russian fairy tales. I wasn't allowed to read them, but if I didn't ask too many questions I could still enjoy making it."

"Huh," Lillith mused, "You know it's a witches house then?"

"No, I didn't," I smiled, "Though that's pretty serendipitous now huh?" I asked her.

"I'd say," Lillith smiled, "It's really cool, I wish I could make something like this."

"Well, maybe Robert and I could show you how to make one at some point? You and Darling could come over and we could show you how it works." I offered.

Lillith smiled wider then, "I'd love that."

"Yeah," Robert said. Now he had finally finished packing stuff up, he was ready to talk. "Why don't we make our shops? We could all work on both and we've got perfect references," Robert gestured around the room, "because we live in them."

"So they'd be like those Victorian miniature houses that matched the real-life house?" Darling said.

"Oh, I love those," Lillith said, bouncing a little with excitement, "Then we could make tiny furniture for them too."

"Well, I don't think we've ever made something so detailed," I said, my hand going to tug at my hair again, "But it would certainly be fun to try."

"Plus, we'd feel like giants," Robert said, as if that was the best part of this project.

I gave him a strange look and he quickly tried to explain himself.

"Well, you know, I like feeling tall," He said, "you know, like when you feel like you're eating trees but it's just broccoli?"

I laughed and that seemed to make Robert look more confused.

"You guys have done that right?" He asked, his voice sounding a little embarrassed.

"We have," Lillith said, "Don't worry Robert."

Robert sighed gratefully and frowned at me to stop giggling at him. I tried my best, but some still escaped as I tried to speak again. "Well, seems like we all have something we can get out of this project." I smiled.

Everyone nodded. We didn't quite know what to say next and it surprised me a little when Darling was the first to speak.

"Does anyone else feel like something is missing since we did the Binding Spell?" She asked, "I keep feeling like I'm forgetting something, or I'm not paying enough attention."

We all thought hard for a moment, and it surprised me more that Robert was the first one of us who replied.

"I don't feel like I've lost something, more like I could get stuck somewhere if I stay still for too long," Robert replied.

Neither of those things seemed to have happened to me, it was strange that we were all having different reactions after the spell. I hadn't particularly felt any different since, though I had had trouble whenever I tried to concentrate on the Grimoire; I got a migraine whenever I tried. I wondered whether I should tell them this or whether I shouldn't because I would have to admit to reading the Grimoire without them.

"I keep feeling like I'm not here," Lillith said after a moment, "Like I'm a ghost, drifting between reality and something else."

"Aww Lil," Darling said, moving out her hand to comfort Lillith.

"No, it's okay," Lillith said, "I'm assuming it's something to do with it being our first spell."

"Are you sure?" I asked. I was worried it might be something other than magic that was making my friends feel this way, though I didn't know what it could be.

"Well, we're not used to how magic affects us yet," Darling said, "maybe we're just hyper-aware of it right now. Like when you wear a different shape of shoes for the first time and you forget how to walk normally?"

"I know that feeling," Robert chimed, "That means that, probably, when we've done a few more spells we'll either get used to it or the feeling will go away."

I nodded, hoping they were right. "That seems like as good an explanation as any," I said, and Lillith gave me a small smile. "Lillith, I wonder if we missed something about setting up for the spell, that made us more sensitive to the magic?"

"We could try looking through the book for more information," Lillith said, "Though given its all in Latin there's a large possibility we did miss something we should have done."

"Actually," I said, not expecting to talk about this so soon, "I haven't told you guys something important about the Grimoire."

"Oh gosh Nav," Lillith said, "Please tell me you didn't throw it away."

"No, I didn't," I said.

"Is there something wrong with it?" Darling asked, "Did it hurt you or something?"

"No no, it's about what's inside it," I explained. "Hang on, let me go get it."

My walking pace sped up so I could get the book quicker, sort of bouncing down the hallway. I had set the book on my dresser a few days ago, and when I went to grab it now I saw the familiar salt ring had appeared around the book again. I didn't know how it kept showing up, or whether the book created the ring by itself, but every time the Grimoire was left unattended for more than a few hours the ring appeared. Grabbing the book from the dresser I walked back into the living room where Lillith, Darling, and Robert were now sitting on the sofa waiting for me.

"Now, this might come as a surprise," I warned them. I sat down in my blue armchair, set the book down on the coffee table in front of all of us, and opened it to the first page about The Elements.

12

The Four Elements Theory

"See, The Elements," I read the title at the top of the page before sitting back in my chair.

"You can read it?" Robert asked.

"Well, yeah, ever since we did the Binding Spell."

Lillith glanced up at me, looking a little hurt, "How much have you read?"

"I haven't been able to read much," I admitted, "I keep getting a headache when I try."

"So you don't know why you can read it?" Darling asked.

"No, I don't," I shrugged, "I'm guessing it's something to do with the magic though, because the page completely changed and I can read it now."

"Why didn't you tell us?" Robert asked, his voice quiet as he frowned at me.

"Well, I just," I realised this might not have been a good idea. "I didn't want to get everyone's hopes up, I keep getting this feeling like I'm missing something about the page that I should have remembered. Also, I wasn't entirely sure if I wanted to keep reading it."

"But you've tried to," Robert said.

I nodded, avoiding his gaze, "I want to know more about the Grimoire, I just can't seem to be able to."

Robert nodded, and I did wonder how upset he was with me. I'd never kept anything from him before, so I understood why he'd be annoyed.

"So, the Elements?" Darling asked.

"Is that why you were asking about them the other day?" Lillith looked up at me.

"Yeah, I kept thinking there should have been five, not four," I explained, "I wondered if you had heard of them to see if the book had gotten the information wrong. Have a read," I gestured to the book.

Lillith, Darling and Robert all peered down at the book, each of them squinting at the words on the page. Robert scrunched up his nose to read the book, but after a moment he looked up at me.

"Nav?" Robert said gently, "I can't read it."

"What?"

"It's still just some weird symbols, I can't read what it says," Robert explained.

"We can't read it either Nav," Darling said, looking at Lillith as well who looked upset.

"You can't?" I asked, looking at Lillith directly.

She shook her head, her eye's a little shiny. "It's still in some other language, maybe Latin, as far as I can tell."

I took the book off the coffee table and looked at the words. It took me a moment to focus but there they were, the same words I'd read after we'd done the Binding Spell.

"The four elements, earth, air, fire, and water, are the fundamental components of magic," I started to read aloud, "that allow magical practitioners to direct their intentions into the world."

I heard Lillith gasp and I looked up.

"So, you can actually read it?" She asked.

"Can you, or are you making it up?" Darling added, frowning at me a little.

Robert leaned over to Darling and shook his head, "Nav doesn't know anything about magic, he couldn't make it up if he tried."

"Well, it seems I'm the only one who can read it," I said, a little annoyed myself at this, "What use is it if I'm the only one who can read it? I mean, I haven't been able to get past these two sentences, that's not very useful."

"Well, you'll have to be designated book reader-witch then," Robert smiled. He got off the sofa then and sat cross-legged on the floor in front of my armchair.

"What?" I asked him.

"Storytime then, Mr. Storyteller," he said, looking the most attentive I'd ever seen him. The girls both copied his pose, sitting cross-legged in front of me with wide eyes. "Go on Nav," Robert said, "We're very curious to know."

"Well, alright then," I said, a little stunned to really argue with him. I felt nervous with the three of them all looking up at me like that, but I looked back down at the book and read some more. "When one of these is unbalanced there is an excess of the element which makes the magic go awry."

"We did have the right elements, didn't we?" Robert asked. "For the Binding Spell I mean."

"We must have," Lillith said, "Nav couldn't read the book otherwise."

"True," Darling nodded, "Though we did have some weird objects in that spell, not exactly what Nav read out from the page. Maybe because the items weren't correct that's why Nav is the only one who can read the book?"

They all waited for me to continue reading, and as I looked down at the page I realised for the first time in days I actually could.

"When one element diminishes another grows to strengthen it, and likewise if one element becomes excessive, nature will compensate. This too can be said of humans, both magical and mundane, and this is where imbalances are felt the strongest. Humans seem to be unique in the world because, while they are of the elements like everything else, they are also connected to one which dominates the personality, actions, thoughts and strengths of the person."

"Does that mean that we have elements?" I asked, looking up from the page.

"Presumably," Robert said.

"I mean, people have been trying to psychologically categorize personality types since society began," Darling said, "That's why some people believe in Zodiac signs and others have Jung personality types. It wouldn't be surprising if witches used elements instead."

"Do you suppose it works?" Robert asked.

"We'll only know if Nav reads some more," Lillith smiled, "Keep reading, it might tell us which elements we are."

"The Earth was created first, and so the elemental nature of it is strong. It houses all other elements, and those connected most to the Earth have a magnetic demeanour and make friends easily. Often social beings, though they find most comfort in a small group of friends, and are fiercely protective of those they care about. Earth elements have a tendency to value the practical, the simple, and the tactile parts of life. They are also the warmest of the elements, kind to a fault, and loyal to the point of excess."

"Well, I know who that is," Darling giggled, and I smiled at her too.

"Who?" Robert asked, looking upset he didn't get the joke.

"You Robert," I said, "It's obviously you."

"Really?" Robert asked, his eyes growing wide.

"I mean, it didn't mention an obsession with strawberry milkshakes, but apart from that it seems pretty accurate."

"Okay," Robert nodded, "I guess I do like sleeping on the floor."

"Exactly!" I said.

"Go on Nav, what's the next one?" Darling asked.

"Water brings life, and with life comes many opportunities to learn. Water elements value knowledge and creativity above all else. They thrive when they follow their curiosity, and when they cannot explore their interests they feel trapped. Often quiet, and they will try their best to know what other people are interested in too. Water elements also tend to have simmering emotions that sometimes get the better of them."

"Huh, now this one I do know," Robert said.

"Yeah, it's like the Grimoire knew Nav was the one reading it," Lillith giggled.

"Well, I'm the only one who can?" I said, quite confused, "What do you mean?"

"Well, curiosity got the better of you," Robert said, "You're reading a magic book that can only be read by you because we did a spell from it and it decided only you could be trusted. If you're not a water element Nav, I don't know who is."

Lillith nodded, "Robert's earth, Nav's water, what's next?" She asked.

"It's air," I replied, looking back down at the book. I wasn't sure I completely agreed with them, but I wanted to keep reading the Grimoire while I could.

"Air is constantly moving, and travels best when loud. Air elements value communication and laughter. They inspire and encourage conversation and are often good storytellers. There is an air of excitement always around these people, and can get them into trouble when they do things impulsively. Air elements are also quick to act and can be good leaders if kept on track."

"Huh, sounds like-," Robert started.

Lillith giggled, "Sounds like you Darl."

"No it doesn't, I mean, I'm not stupid," Darling said, starting to blush.

"It doesn't say you are," Robert said, trying to sound reassuring, "It didn't say anything about being stupid, it was the opposite Darling."

"Yeah," I said, "It just seems to me that it's saying you're more likely to learn by talking to people, rather than reading books."

"And that's how we used to study at school," Lillith added, "We used to talk through subjects and you used to understand concepts far easier once I explained them to you."

"That's true," Darling said, seeming to calm down. "That just leaves Lillith then."

"Fire was the final element created, and took years for people to tame to harness it's power. The fire element, as it exists in humans, also takes years to harness. In most cases, the fire element does not consume the person's character permanently, but instead comes and goes throughout a person's lifetime. Fire, instead of blazing constantly in a person, is something that may grow within them or be brought out with particular emotions. The fire element may be fuelled by a particular person, who angers, annoys, confuses, or even inspires another into acting passionately, or aggressively. Often when a person is influenced by the fire element, they are consumed with a singular emotion. The fire element may also inspire a person, may encourage them to act upon something they are passionate about, or might push them to act strongly without thinking."

"Well, that doesn't sound like Lillith at all," I said, looking up from the book. Lillith's cheeks went pink when I said it so matter-of-factly.

"I don't know, some of it sounds about right," Darling said. "She did inspire me to be more myself in high school, and she got Nav excited to learn about magic.

"I wouldn't say I'm exactly passionate about magic yet though," I added.

"I was thinking that Lillith sounded like a bit of all the elements," Robert offered, looking at Lillith gently, "You seem to be on the edge of all of them."

"Of course," Lillith laughed a little, "Difficult to define, that's what I've always strived to be. Besides, every system has outliers, its no wonder that one of us doesn't fit a mold."

"That's true," I nodded. "It just doesn't seem fair that we all can see ourselves in an element and you can't."

"Oh, that's fine," Lillith waved at me, "I'm happy being an enigma. Maybe that means that I just haven't made a strong enough connection to an element yet?" She was trying to hide it, but I could tell she was a little upset she didn't fit perfectly into an element.

"It would make sense," I said, "Besides, this is just one magical book too, who says it's the be-all and end-all of magic? We don't have to follow every word."

Lillith looked a bit happier at that.

"Do you guys want me to keep reading? There's nothing more about the elements on this page, but we could try something else?" I asked.

"Actually," Lillith said, stretching her legs, "both my feet have gone to sleep and I think that's a pretty good place to stop for now. We all should probably think about our elements and just get used to the idea."

I nodded in agreement, "This is the furthest I've read so far, and I definitely need some time to think about it."

"But we'll have another story time soon?" Robert asked

as he helped Lillith and Darling stand up again. I shut the Grimoire and put it under my arm, ready to put it back away in my bedroom.

"Sure," I told him, "I wonder if we notice more magical changes, now we're aware of our elements?"

"Yeah," Darling smiled, "We can keep an eye out for things now."

13

A Protection Net?

That afternoon Robert and I were hanging out in The Velvet Mansion. We weren't technically open, but I'd found that looking through the strange antiques that collected in the shop was a fun past-time, even when we weren't working. Robert was sitting at the front counter, a pair of aviator goggles on his head as he fiddled with the gears of a clock.

When we all were reading the Grimoire this morning it had reminded me of something, but I'd already forgotten what I was looking for by the time Robert and I had gone downstairs. Currently I was looking through the collection of dusty jewellery boxes, opening each of them to see whether any special trinkets were inside. Thinking about the medal Lillith had showed me, I wondered how many covens might be in Ebonwick. How many witches might be gathering to-gether to make spells and push them out into the world. One day, I thought, I might even be part of one. I knew that Robert and Lillith both thought that we already were our own little coven, but we didn't have a proper leader, and apart from our very limited knowledge of witchcraft, we didn't know anything about that world.

"Find any?" Robert asked. I looked up over the set of drawers that hid me from Robert's view at the counter.

"Not a one," I said, "I guess Lillith was right, they don't just get thrown out for anyone to find."

"And if anyone was going to find one, it would be us," Robert nodded.

"Do you really think we could be in a coven? With the girls?" I asked, crossing my legs on the floor and leaning back on my hands.

"I really don't know," Robert shrugged, "I mean, we've only done one spell so far. That doesn't usually make you a coven."

"That's true." My chest felt almost hollow though I could feel my heart beating through my palms. Something about the idea of covens and more spells was bothering me a little. I almost wished we knew an experienced witch to be our teacher, but at the same time I didn't really want anyone else to be part of our group of four. The dread that my parents might find out and come looking for me too caused a clawing feeling in my stomach.

"I guess that's the whole idea," Robert mused, and I was confused at first what he meant but he kept talking. "Witchcraft isn't something you can really learn all about from a book, or even lots of books. You have to do it, experiment, see what works." He looked at me with an interesting expression. I could tell he was excited about the concept of witchcraft, but this was overshadowed by another feeling that I couldn't quite decipher in his face.

"Do you think that's what we should do then?" I asked, my tone hesitant because I wasn't quite sure I should be saying this out loud. "Experiment some more with some spells?"

"I suppose, if we picked the right ones," the corner of Robert's mouth curled up into an optimistic smile, "I don't think it would be any great tragedy to just try a few."

I stood up straight now, some of my hair falling forward. I hadn't put as much product in it this morning as I normally did and it was really fluffy. "You think so? Do you know what we should try next?" I asked.

"Well, I was thinking about it," he said. He suddenly got up from his seat and made his way over to me, leaning on the chest of drawers that was in front of me. "In the Bard's Tales, they talk about putting something called a 'protection net' around the city. It protects the place from magical attacks I think, and really evil people can't walk through the net."

"So it's like a dome over the city?" I asked.

"Yeah," Robert smiled, "I guess so."

"How do they do it?" I asked. Something about the idea of some form of magical protection sounded good to me. I even wondered whether it would mean my parents couldn't find out that I was learning about magic too.

"They make this powder," Robert said, frowning a little to remember, "I don't think it actually says what the ingredients are, but they sprinkle the powder a little way out from the city, and it creates an unbroken ring."

"Wait," my eyes widened as I realised something, "It wasn't made of salt, was it?"

"Maybe?" Robert said, "It does say that the grass dies where the powder was put, and salt does that. But I'm sure there was more to it than that."

"Robert, the Grimoire," I said, my heart beating fast now. Not from nerves either, this time from excitement. "Every time I leave the Grimoire somewhere a salt ring appears around it."

"Protecting itself?" Robert asked, "From what?"

"Presumably from people who might use it for the wrong reasons," I said. "Remember when it first appeared on the dining table?"

Robert nodded.

"I had this feeling that it wanted to be read, but I went all weird when you tried to read it-,"

"Weirder than usual," Robert said, "Do you think it knew that you were the only one that could read it?"

"Maybe it only wants me to read it, that's why I'm the only one who can?" I asked.

"It did appear on the table without either of us having a key to the cabinet," Robert said, "and the only page we could read before was the Binding Spell."

"Binding it to what?" I asked, "Binding it to me so I can read it?"

"Or binding it to the coven? It wouldn't surprise me if it knows exactly who has enough magic to use it properly," Robert said. "And maybe it's protecting itself because we haven't been doing that yet?"

"Maybe," I nodded, getting up off the floor now and dusting myself off. "Do you think we should look in it for a, what was it?"

"A protection net?" Robert said, "Though we could see if it has anything about magical protection in it to start."

"Right," I nodded, a smile growing on my face the more I thought about it. "I'm going to go get the Grimoire and bring it down, we can look through it and see if we can find something similar."

"The Bard's Tales are in my satchel anyway," Robert waved to the coat stand next to the counter. "I'm going to get some muffins from The Last Drop while you get the Grimoire."

"Thanks Robert," I smiled, "I'll make tea then and get us a spot to go through the books."

"Excellent choice," Robert said, grabbing his coat. "What muffin do you want?"

"Well, I can't have one of Mammy's macadamia and caramel ones," I said, making Robert laugh, "So I guess a spinach one?"

"I'll see what they have," Robert smiled, "Oh, Darling bought me a new mug to replace the smashed one, you can make my tea in that now."

"Yes boss," I said, giving him a little salute as he left through the door to The Velvet Mansion and walked up into the street. After I saw him go I started up the stairs to collect the book and make tea.

14

Two Books, Two Boys, and Study Muffins

I put the kettle on before I made my way to my bedroom to fetch the Grimoire. This time I'd put it on one of the shelves in my wardrobe, and I saw the familiar salt ring had appeared around it as I went to pick it up.

"Now," I said quietly to the book as I held it up, "If I put some protection spell around the flat, will you please stop making a mess?"

The Grimoire didn't move or say anything, and I didn't really expect it too. I giggled a little as I put it under my arm and shook my head. "I'm talking to a book now, as my brother always suspected I would end up doing."

I tucked the book under my arm and headed back to the kitchen, where I could hear the kettle was close to boiling already. I set the book on the dining table before turning around to retrieve two mugs from the cupboard above the kettle. I saw my favourite one instantly, a mug that I perceived to be the king of the mugs that I owned. It was a large ceramic mug I'd picked up at one of Ebonwick's Christmas markets a few years ago, handmade, and decorated with a skull that looked like it had the moon in it's forehead. It must have been a leftover from the Halloween markets, which I had not been allowed to go to. I took it down and placed it on the kitchen bench before looking up again to find Robert's new mug. I had smashed his favourite one recently, when he'd tried to read the Grimoire and I'd fallen on it. It had been a pretty cool mug, with a red polka dot pattern and a griffin painted on it.

The new mug was still in its non-descript white box I realised, and I took the box out of the cupboard to unpack it on the bench. I lifted the mug up and smiled. Of course, Darling had found something this perfect. The mug was tall and had a print on it that made it look like a pink strawberry milkshake, and the handle was a stack of strawberries. I put the box back into the cupboard and placed some teabags into the mugs. Robert and I drank different teas, it was something that we never had agreed on because we grew up with such different flavours. Robert's parents liked really sweet tea that usually had honeycomb already in the tea bags. I had no idea where they got it from, Robert had never told me, but we now had a permanent jar of the honeycomb tea in our flat. My parents always had black tea, as black and strong and hot as they could make it. Robert used to joke that they needed it so black to match the colour of their souls. I liked strong tea but I still had milk in mine, though not as much as Robert did. Robert's tea always came out looking like the colour of sponge cake, whereas mine was usually a comforting 'teddy bear brown' colour.

Once I'd finished making both mugs of tea I carried them downstairs to The Velvet Mansion. I set them on the counter to make sure I could find them again and looked around the shop for a comfy spot that Robert and I could use to do our research. It was amazing how quickly things seemed to move around the place when Robert and I were usually the only ones in here most the time. I found a spot at the back of the shop, two lumpy looking armchairs that had been set down next to a glass cabinet full of books. I moved closer to make sure we could actually fit in between the furniture that crowded the walkway to the spot. As I got closer my attention focused on the glass cabinet. I'd first seen the Green Grimoire in that cabinet, propped forward like the jewel in a display case. It was still locked as far as I knew, but the space the Grimoire had sat was now replaced with a stack of books so old the covers were barely keeping them together. The cabinet looked a little dusty now too, probably because I had refused to go near it when the Grimoire had started moving around.

I found a small coffee table close by to the armchairs and moved that, so we had somewhere to put our tea, then bounced back upstairs to get the book off the dining table. By the time I was coming back down the stairs Robert had returned, coming into the shop and taking his coat off.

"Is it getting colder outside?" I asked.

"The wind is definitely picking up," he said, producing

a box from his coat, "I think we're going to have a colder autumn than normal."

"Oh yes," I smiled, "That'll be good."

"There you go again," Robert said, teasing me a little, "Not all of us can resist the cold as well as you Nav."

"Maybe that's just part of my magical witch powers." I said, wiggling my fingers at him as I moved to where I'd set up our reading spot. "Over here, follow your tea-seeking nose." I said to him.

He placed his hands on his hips and bent over so his nose was pointing in front of him like a hunting dog. I laughed at him a little, he looked a bit like a cartoon, following his nose. I watched him walk like this until he got to the armchairs, where he stood up and waited for me to join him.

"Right," I said, setting the Grimoire down on the table. I sat down in the taller of the two chairs so I could spread out a bit and grabbed my mug from the coffee table. "So, where do you think we should start?" I asked.

"I'll look through the Bard's Tales," Robert said, "Try and find a description of the protection net. You can flick through the Grimoire for protection magic I guess? See if it says anything about protecting buildings and stuff like that, if we even need it."

I nodded. My parents had been so against the notion of magic, of every kind, and it hadn't occurred to me that there might be things that magic needed to be protected from. It seemed a little strange that witches could fear things, but I guessed that if people could be afraid of magic, then magic could be afraid of things too. I watched Robert sip his pale, toffee sweet tea and flick through his little copy of the Bard's Tales. His mum, Mammy, had gotten a new copy of the Tales printed and bound for Robert when we'd moved out of home, so that the family's old copy could stay at Robert's parent's house until it was time to hand it down. Robert's copy was very nice, the papers were edged with gold and the leather binding was a warm red-magenta colour. The cover was engraved with an acoustic guitar, the kind that Robert had played in high school, and had the title burnt into the leather. I felt a pang of jealousy that he had such a nice family heirloom to look through, while I ran my hands over the Grimoire.

"You alright Nav?" Robert asked, noticing I was staring over at him.

"Yeah, just thinking," I said. "I wish my family had anything old."

My parent's house was the epitome of 'new is always better'. We always had new appliances, new fixtures, new technology, new textbooks. A lot of the time my mother hadn't even let me borrow books out from the library, as soon as I mentioned something I wanted to read she would buy it outright. That was part of the reason I had sought out The Velvet Mansion I supposed. A building full of furniture with a story, a history, a life that was older than a few years. I had craved it my whole life.

"Well, that's not your fault," Robert said, "I mean, your parents have really good jobs and they always liked new things."

I nodded, "At least I got to go to your house and soak up all the old things."

"Do you remember when Mammy thought I'd stolen that pair of boots? The ones you got for my birthday?" Robert smiled.

"She couldn't believe my parents had agreed to buy them for you," I smiled back.

"I wish I still had them sometimes," Robert said, taking off his shoes so he could sit in his chair more comfortably. "They had those metal caps on the toes, and I felt so cool."

"Oh I remember that," I said, "you were so excited that they made a proper thumping noise on the floor because they were so heavy."

"I'd buy a pair again if I knew where to find them," Robert said, "They were a good pair of boots."

I nodded, thinking I should remember that and see if I could find Robert a pair. I looked down at the Grimoire and opened the front cover, noticing all the small pairs of initials that I'd seen the first time I'd opened it. They didn't look as confusing as the first time though, most were almost legible. I wondered if the Grimoire was letting me see them more clearly this time. Lillith had guessed they had been all the previous owners of the Grimoire, and the signatures came in a range of styles. Some were neat, some messy, some were ink, some were pen or pencil, and some had been smudged a little so you couldn't really tell what the letter's were. I entertained the brief thought that one day I could write my own initials in the cover, but I wondered if that might be rude because I hadn't been passed down the book from one of the other people.

I started looking at each page in the Grimoire from the start, trying to read the titles of the pages to find anything about magical protection. The page about the four elements was pretty close to the beginning, and then there were title pages on each element separately. After those there were titles about the seasons, the planets, and one about the phases of the moon.

"I found it," Robert said, placing his book on the coffee table so I could look at it too.

I looked down to read the passage Robert was pointing to. The words had been printed with a brown ink that made me smile again at how personal and special this book must be to Robert.

The young man crushed up the ingredients for the protective net that we would sprinkle around the town tonight. Spice from the sea, the cages of the unborn, the extinguished dust of the night's sun, and some leaves from the creeping floor of the rose. Once the mixture was crushed and combined together so that no one could identify the separate ingredients, the powder was distributed between the five of us...

"Wow," I said, "I didn't think it would actually give us some ingredients."

"Thing is, this part of the Tales was written by Eadwine, who lived in the Medieval era," Robert said, "I don't know whether we'll still be able to actually get any of those ingredients, even if we can figure out what they are."

"You're right," I nodded, thinking a little. I looked back down at the Grimoire and I had an idea. Once or twice, when I'd tried to open the book at a random page, it had fallen open at the exact page I needed. I wondered whether I could try and do that again, but this time on purpose to find the page about protection magic. "I'm going to try something," I said to Robert as I shut the book.

I closed my eyes and held the book up a little, aiming it so that it would hopefully open up as it fell into my lap. I took a few deep breaths in, thinking about the protection spell in Robert's story book and hoping there was something similar the Grimoire could show me. After counting to three in my head I dropped the book and it thudded into my lap.

15

The Circle and The Witch Next Door

I opened one of my eyes cautiously, looking over at Robert first. His head was tilted to one side and his brows were curled up in a confused expression. I glanced down at the pages the Grimoire had fallen open on. On the left was a page about salt, and the right page was titled 'The Circle'. I stared at the page a bit closer, it looked like one of the oldest pages, and the handwriting was quite messy compared to the Binding Spell I had read before. It seemed to be set up with a few simple illustrations that showed the process, like in a recipe book where the pictures follow the instructions.

"This looks like a more complicated spell," I told Robert, "It's more than just reading the words, its like a recipe."

"Alright," Robert said, shuffling a little in his armchair so he could lean closer to me. "Does it say what it's used for, why would witches need to make a circle?"

"Good question," I said. I looked at the top of the page where the writing was larger, as if whoever wrote the page had gotten better at writing the further down the page they were. I started to read the passage at the top of the page, running my finger under the words so I didn't lose my place.

In order to keep ourselves protected from those that would discover our magic and wish to harm us, witches must cast a protective circle invisible to those who have no magic. The circle must be performed at the witching hour, in order to assure secrecy.

"Well, I already have several questions," Robert said as I paused.

"Me too," I said, "Who do you think would want to harm witches?"

"Your parents come to mind," Robert said, "I wonder what the witching hour is?"

I nodded. My parents were exactly the type of people the Grimoire would warn against. They hated magic, didn't want anything to do with it. They'd confiscated books I'd brought home from the school library and drawings I'd done as a small child that they suspected might inspire me to learn about magic. Even creatures associated with magic, like unicorns, were seen as 'too magical' to exist in their house, even as a story.

"I think we need to go visit Lillith and Darling," I said, looking at the page, "This seems a little too complicated for us."

"Well, not too complicated," Robert said, trying to make me feel a bit better, "We still don't know most the basics of magic yet, so we need to ask someone who does."

"Should we go over now?" I asked. I was excited to see the girls again, but Robert made a strange face.

"Wait, what's this bit?" Robert asked, pointing a bit further down the page where the illustrations started. I read further down, finding that part of the page.

Mix the ingredients and spread the protection powder around the area, walking clockwise and reciting the four elements to ask their protection over the space.

"What ingredients?" Robert asked, opening the Bard's Tales to the page he'd marked earlier.

I scanned the page, looking for what we'd need to make the 'protection powder' for the circle. I frowned and scanned the page again. I looked up at Robert, my stomach sinking a little. "There isn't any," I said, "Maybe they're on a different page but," my voice dropped away as I thought of something.

"What's wrong?" Robert asked.

"Maybe this is why witches come in families, like Lillith was telling me about her great-grandmother," I said, "Some of the spells might be handed down, and the ingredients would be family recipes that never get written down, so they can't be stolen or used by someone outside the family."

"You think every witch might have different ingredients they use?" Robert asked.

"Every family might," I said, "That means that we can't do this spell though, we don't know the ingredients."

"Makes sense then," Robert said, "why the Bard's Tales gives the ingredients like a riddle."

"It wasn't meant to be instructions," I nodded, "Not really, that knowledge was meant for that warlock-,"

"Maybe we could answer the riddle though?" Robert offered.

"That, or find a family of witches." I said, a bit disgruntled that we hadn't found anything useful yet.

"Right, I think we do need to go see Lillith now," Robert said, "Maybe her great-grandmother taught her the ingredients."

"Though, if each family has a different recipe for the spell, then wouldn't her family have had completely different ingredients?"

"Well, if it's a family recipe then it could still work, though I do think we need help working out this riddle anyway."

"Yeah," I said, smiling a little, "We're not at a dead-end yet."

"Come on," Robert said, picking up his coat from the back of the chair.

"Alright," I stood up too, "I'll get my jacket, the rain looks a bit strong today."

Robert looked up at the high windows and made a face like he was thinking hard. "Yeah, it's almost whipping now, best get the leather jacket."

"Should we bring an umbrella?" I asked while he was at the window.

"Don't think so," Robert shook his head, "the wind is too strong, might break it."

I picked up the Grimoire while Robert grabbed the Bard's Tales. I made my way through The Velvet Mansion back towards the stairs that led to our flat. I stepped quickly through the flat to my room, where my closet was already open and some clothes were spilling out as usual. I grabbed my leather jacket off the hanger and slipped it on before heading back downstairs to where Robert was waiting by the front door of The Velvet Mansion.

"To the witch next door!" Robert said, opening the front door of The Velvet Mansion so we could walk out.

I giggled a little, walking past him and letting Robert lock the front door. I covered the Grimoire with my jacket, sheltering it from the rain. I was excited to see the girls again, even more when I felt the rain falling on my face and stinging a little. After Robert had locked the door to the antiques store we both started walking briskly towards Grey and Hallward next door.

16

Gray and Hallward

While we'd visited next door a lot since Robert and I had moved into The Velvet Mansion, we rarely got to hang out in Grey and Hallward with Lillith and Darling. It was an art supplies store, and we hadn't seen it since it had been renovated. I opened the door and heard the bells jingle, making me smile at the tinkling sound. Darling looked up from the front counter and beamed at us.

"Hi Robert, Nav," She smiled, though her focus was mostly on Robert. "Lillith is doing a coffee run, what's happened?"

I felt a little upset that Lillith wasn't there too, but I knew she would be back soon. Most of the time if we were working, we got our coffee from The Last Drop on the corner of our street, and she wouldn't be too long coming back.

"Actually, we've been looking at something," I started.

"We were thinking about the Binding Spell, how we all felt

kinda strange after it, and we wondered whether we'd missed something when we did it." Robert explained.

"Yeah," I nodded, "we found a kind of protection spell, but it's missing some details that we wanted Lillith's help to figure it out."

"Oh, cool," Darling smiled, "Sounds like fun, is there anything I can do to help?"

"Are you any good at riddles?" Robert asked.

"Pretty good, with a little time," She replied.

I watched Robert get the Bard's Tales out of his jacket and lay it on the counter, opening it to the pink ribbon he'd used to mark his place. He pointed at the passage with the ingredients riddle that we'd read before, and let Darling read it.

I took a moment to look around the shop a bit, taking in all the art supplies. My hands tingled slightly, wanting to touch the brushes I could see on a large rack. I hadn't made anything for a while, and I missed the feeling of holding tools in my hands and just, creating. Robert and I used to work together to make things, but we hadn't since we'd moved into The Velvet Mansion. Too much time being adults I supposed, though I did miss building miniatures like we used to. We had planned with Lillith and Darling to make some replicas of our flats, and I was excited for that. Maybe I could even treat myself with some tiny new sculpting tools to make the little objects around our flats.

I looked over at Robert and Darling, bent over the Bard's Tales book together. They sort of matched, in a strange way. Well, maybe not matched, but they definitely suited each other. They were practically touching foreheads looking at the book. Darling's hair was short and looked like it was tickling

Robert's nose, but he was trying really hard not to sneeze. Robert's hair was getting longer, and he'd started wearing it up more often, though he hadn't quite mastered the 'man bun' look yet. There were strands of his curly hair coming out all over the place, but it made him look soft and friendly.

Darling looked up a little and noticed me watching them. Her cheeks grew pink and she quickly tucked a strand of hair behind her ear. I smiled, looking towards the door as the bells jingled again. Lillith was struggling a little, carrying a tray of four large takeaway cups of coffee. I stepped closer to hold the door open for her so she wouldn't drop anything.

"Hey Lillith," I smiled.

"Hi Nav, hey Robert," she said, bringing the coffee cups over to the front counter. "I brought everyone coffee, I didn't expect you two to already be here."

"They came over just after you left," Darling said, picking up the coffee cup with her name on it, "They wanted your help with a spell I think."

"Yes," I blurted out, "Please, we found something-,"

"We're just missing pieces," Robert said.

"Alright, well, coffee first," Lillith laughed quietly, "Robert, I saw something different on the menu I thought you might like." She passed us each a coffee cup, and I waited for Robert to try his.

Robert took a tentative sip, before smiling and taking a proper drink from his coffee cup. Robert had never really liked coffee, as far as I knew, he only ever drank it when he was too tired to taste the flavour. "What is it?" I asked.

"I don't know but its amazing," Robert smiled.

Lillith giggled, "Apparently it's a strawberry roasted

coffee," she smiled, "I don't know how they made it, but it tastes more like strawberries and it's not too strong."

"That sounds really cool," I smiled, taking a sip of my own coffee. It was a creamier caramel latte than I was used to, but it was delicious.

"So," Lillith said after a moment, "What's this spell you found?"

"Well, we actually found two," I said, "though we're not quite sure, it might be the same one."

"We think that the Bard's Tales actually has some spells in it, but disguised," Robert added.

"Alright, so we've got two spells that might be connected, but you haven't explained why," Lillith said. She looked at me a little confused, and I had the feeling that she was upset we'd been looking up spells without her again.

"We were thinking about the Binding Spell, and how we all felt really strange after it," I said.

"And we all blacked out, except you," Robert added.

"We wondered whether there was some kind of protection spell we should have done first, and Robert remembered something from the Bard's Tales."

"In it, they place a mixture around the city to protect it from things that could harm magic," Robert explained with a shrug.

"And I looked through the Grimoire and found there's a spell called 'The Circle' that explains the same process, but doesn't give any ingredients," I told her. "We came to a dead end, and I thought that maybe the ingredients were a secret passed through families-,"

"That you might know from your great-grandmother?" Robert asked.

Lillith was nodding in understanding to everything we said, until Robert finished. Then she started to think and her eyebrows furrowed a little. "I'm sorry Nav, I don't remember anything about a protective circle."

My stomach dropped a little, though I tried not to show my disappointment too much.

"Hang on," Darling said, "Lillith, what are medieval spices?" she looked at Lillith excitedly.

"Black pepper, ginger, saffron, cinnamon, and salt I think," Lillith replied.

"Salt?" I asked.

"Back then salt gave flavour to food, and not many people had the ability to go to the sea to get some," Lillith replied, "so it would have been considered a spice by the people who'd never tried it."

"That's what I was thinking," Darling said, "spice from the sea,"

"What do you mean?" I asked.

"It's here, in the Bard's Tales," Darling pointed, "Spice from the sea, the cages of the unborn, the extinguished dust of the night's sun, and some leaves from the creeping floor of the rose."

"A riddle of ingredients, covered up by medieval under-standing," Lillith's eyes grew wide, "So, spice from the sea-,"

"Sea salt," Darling smiled.

"That's a start," I grinned, "I wonder if we could figure out the rest?"

"Cages of the unborn," Robert said, "What in Ebonwick does that mean?"

"Oh my gosh," Lillith's nose twitched a little, like it did whenever she remembered something. "I know what it is, hang on." She put her coffee cup on the counter and made her way to the back of the shop. There was a curtain hiding the staircase that led to Lillith and Darling's flat upstairs, and that's where she disappeared.

"What do you think it is?" Robert asked.

"I don't know," Darling said, "but we've got a whole kitchen cupboard full of strange things she's collected over the years."

"Like what?" Robert asked.

"Like, dried flowers, pebbles, seed pods, shells, really obscure cooking herbs and so much tea you'd think she was going to open a teahouse." Darling explained.

Lillith's footsteps could be heard coming quickly back down the steps and she seemed to fly back towards us with a large jar in her hands.

"What is it?" I asked.

"My sister always used to make this joke," Lillith said. She showed us the label on the front of the jar that read 'the cages of the unborn'.

"Is that eggshells?" Darling asked, looking at the fine brown and white chips inside the jar Lillith was holding.

"It is," Lillith said, placing the jar on the counter, "My grandmother and mother always had a jar of eggshells in the house, I remember my mother telling me they were good food for plants and you should always have some just in case."

"Why would they be in a protection spell then?" I asked, "I didn't think your mum did any witchcraft."

"She doesn't," Lillith said, "That's why I thought it was a bit strange, but I decided to start keeping eggshells just in case."

"That's why you asked us for ours," I exclaimed, remembering Robert telling me a few days ago.

"Yeah, I suddenly felt this need for them." Lillith explained. "Anyway, we have two of the ingredients for the protection spell now."

"Why eggshells?" Robert asked, "I mean, they break so easily, that doesn't seem very 'protecting'."

"Eggshells are supposed to protect what's inside them, allowing them to grow until they can protect themselves," Darling suggested.

"That does make sense," I said, watching Robert nod.

"What's the next one?" Lillith asked.

"Extinguished dust of the night's sun," Darling read from the book.

"The night's sun?" I asked.

"Well, we're talking about the medieval period," Darling said, "so the night's sun could be a wooden torch?"

"But you don't extinguish those," Robert said, "they burn out."

"And you'd need to catch the 'extinguished dust'," I said.

"Oh," Darling said, "Lillith, that experiment we did at school."

"Which one?" Lillith asked.

"We had a candle, and a glass," Darling explained, "and we had to extinguish the flame with the glass and then measure how much soot we could collect, depending on the height of the flame."

"Oh yeah," Lillith said, "Why did we do that again?"

"Didn't have anything better planned," Darling shrugged, "Anyway, do you think that's the clue? Soot from a candle?"

"Extinguished dust," I thought.

"From the night's sun," Robert finished, smiling over at Darling, "I'd say a candle is our best bet."

"And the last one, it sounds like something from a gardening book," Darling said, "leaves from the creeping floor of the rose. But roses don't generally 'creep'."

"And even less on the floor," Lillith shook her head.

"Oh, hang on," Robert said, "Mammy uses a herb in her garden, it crawls along the floor and makes a kind of carpet."

"What's that called again?" I asked.

"It's actually a type of rosemary," Robert said.

"Floor of the rose," Darling mused, "That's why it's not talking about flowers, it's not a true rose plant." She beamed at Robert, and Lillith and I couldn't help looking at each other and giggling.

"Right, Lillith," I said, "Have you got any rosemary?"

"Of course, she does," Darling smiled, "Lillith always has rosemary."

"I use it in shortbread sometimes," Lillith smiled at me.

"Wow, I'd like to try that," I said. I thought for a moment, turning to Robert, "I wonder if you can put magic in food?"

"Well, I bet Mammy can," Robert said.

I nodded, "If anyone can put magic in food it's Mammy. Lillith, maybe your shortbread would be a good protection spell we could eat?"

"We could try," Lillith smiled, "though I think maybe doing the protection circle would be more helpful first."

Robert nodded this time, "Well, we know the ingredients now, we can work out the rest of the spell."

"Right, seems like we need to plan another movie night and work this spell out," Darling said, clapping her hands, "Nav, Robert, you guys can come to ours tonight. Though I do think we need to tidy up first."

"Oh yeah," Lillith said, looking a little guilty.

"That's alright, we should really get back to The Velvet Mansion anyway," I said, "just in case we get a customer."

"Alright," Lillith smiled, "We'll see you two tonight then?"

"See you tonight," Robert gave her and Darling a wide grin. We gathered up our books and our coffee cups and headed out of the shop.

17

Itchy Mittens and the Magic Mascot

As we walked back to The Velvet Mansion, I remembered what I'd been looking for earlier, and I stopped to ask Robert about it.

"Hey," I said, "You know that skull we had when we did the Binding Spell? Where did it go?"

"I don't remember," Robert said, "Do you think Lillith took it?"

"She was the only one who touched it," I said, "But I remember it still being in the basement when I cleaned up after the spell."

"So it should still be here," Robert opened the door to the Velvet Mansion and I followed him in quickly. "Do you want to check the basement?"

"Yeah, I think so," I nodded, "I feel like we should bring it with us tonight."

"I think so too," Robert agreed, "It can be our little magic mascot." He smiled, taking his coat off and moving towards the front counter.

"Can I borrow your lighter?" I asked, picking up a candle from the large chest near the front counter. "I'll head down there now, see if I can find the skull."

"Alright," Robert said, producing the lighter from his trouser pocket, "You want me to come too?"

"No, I should be alright," I said, lighting the candle wick and waiting a moment for the flame to grow. "Just stay at the top of the trap door for me?" I asked him. I'd been in the basement a couple of times now, but I still wasn't fond of how dark it was down there. And because this time I was going to be looking for a human skull, I wanted Robert close by just in case.

"Sure," Robert said, walking over to the ugly carpet that hid the basement trap door he'd found a few weeks ago. He lifted the carpet with his foot before grabbing the door handle and pulling it open so I could go down the stairs.

"Don't let the door close," I warned, giving Robert a look.

"Of course not," Robert shook his head, "That would be cruel, I'm not Christopher."

I nodded. Robert was the opposite of his twin brother Christopher. Christopher was tall and built like a brick wall, and he took every opportunity to pick on people that were smaller than him, especially Robert. He had claimed once that he only did it so Robert could defend himself against 'real bullies' but we'd never met any of those 'real bullies' he claimed were out to get us all those years. Robert and Christopher had barely spoken a sentence to each other in at least 5 years, and I helped Robert avoid his brother as best I could.

"You're right," I said, starting to walk down the stairs to the basement, "I'll call out if I need help."

"I'll come running," Robert nodded.

I walked down the dark stairs, hearing a few creaks as I got to the bottom. The light of the candle was just enough for me to see in front of myself but wasn't strong enough to light up the room. I wondered for a moment if I should light some of the candles that were stored in the basement, but I didn't really want to be down here for that long to need them. Even though we'd done the Binding Spell in the basement, it was still not a comforting place, and I didn't really want to be in the basement unless I really had to.

I moved the candle around me, trying to get its light to reveal where the skull might be. After walking around in a circle and moving the candle back and forth across the room, I realised that the skull wasn't here. I let out a disappointed sigh, it must have been loud enough for Robert to hear upstairs because he called down to me.

"You didn't find it?" He asked.

"No," I called back, making my way back up the stairs, "It must be somewhere in the store, I just can't remember where I would have put it."

"Lillith might have taken it home?" Robert offered. I'd reached the trap door now and was climbing out of it.

"I don't know," I said, "At least we're going over there tonight, we can ask."

Robert nodded, "Do you want me to have a look around the store, just in case you saw it but didn't realise?"

"If you want," I shrugged, trying to get some of the dust off me. "You might not find it but it'd make me feel better if you can't either."

"How's that?" Robert asked, giving me a helpful pat before he started moving slowly around some of the antiques, looking for the skull.

"Well, I'm usually very observant of these things," I said, "it annoys me when I can't find stuff."

"Sometimes you get too preoccupied by a single thought though," Robert reminded me, "Remember when you first started collecting blue things, and then I asked you to find me a red ribbon and you couldn't find it because your mind was still on blue?"

"It was right in front of me," I nodded. I sat down at the front counter of The Velvet Mansion and watched Robert looking through the antiques.

"Exactly," Robert said, "You were probably just thinking of something else and it took over. You did forget what you were looking for the first time you looked for the skull."

"I started looking for medallions," I remembered, "Even when I started looking for the skull, I was still thinking about them."

"There you go," Robert smiled, "See? No point getting upset about not seeing something."

"I guess so," I shifted a little in the chair.

"You thinking about the protection circle?" Robert asked, noticing I'd gone quiet.

"No, actually," I said, "Thinking about Lillith's family."

"What about?" Robert asked.

"She's so lucky," I started, "She has magic in her blood, I mean, she knows things from her great-grandmother that I wasn't even allowed to think about until a few weeks ago."

"Well, you can think about it now," Robert said, "And pass it down, you can be the great-grandmother witch to someone else if you want."

I laughed a little at the thought. "Right, because I'd make an awesome great-grandmother witch," I joked.

"Of course, you would," Robert giggled, "Grey head of hair in a neat bun, knitting needles carved with magical symbols so every woolly jumper was knitted with an anti-itching spell."

"If I ever start knitting, I want you to burn everything I make," I said seriously. My grandmother used to knit, the one on my mother's side that had raised my brother Morgan the first few years of his life. In those short 6 years she'd knitted me three jumpers and at least a dozen pairs of mittens, all of which were ghastly colours and always seemed to make me break out in a rash that looked more like second-degree burns. I still had a strange looking white patch on my hands that looked like the opposite of a birthmark from the amount of cream I'd had to put on them.

"Don't worry Nav," Robert said, "I promise if I see you even looking at a ball of wool I'll shake you."

"Shake me?" I asked, letting a scoff escape my throat. It didn't sound like much of a threat.

Robert turned to look me in the eyes and held his hands

in the air. He made a shaking motion with his hands as he stared at me and said, "Vigorously."

I couldn't help laughing at him, and I watched him smile before he kept looking around the shop.

"So, do you think you'd be really different if you had a witch family?" Robert asked.

"Are you kidding?" I asked, "I'd be completely different. I'd probably be running a magical art gallery where the paintings move and own a flat that did the cleaning for me by now."

"I don't know," Robert shrugged, "I mean, do you think you'd be happier?"

"I might be less frightened of my own family," I said, "But, on the other hand I might not have met you either, and I don't think I would prefer that."

"Well, that does make me feel a little better," Robert said, "I do think you might have left Ebonwick by now though."

"Maybe," I nodded. I'd had plans to travel after I left high school, but I still didn't know half as much about Ebonwick as I wanted to yet. And now that I'd started learning about magic in the town too, I was too curious about what else I might find. Robert did have a point though. If I already knew about the magic in Ebonwick, I might have been more excited to travel and find the magic in other places too.

"I'd want you to come with me though," I said to Robert.

"I'd be happy to accompany you," Robert smiled. I heard him shift something heavy, before he made a satisfied sigh. "There you are you rogue." He said.

"What?" I asked.

Robert held up the skull that we'd used during the Binding Spell. "I found it," he said, sounding pleased with himself.

"Finally," I said, "where was it?"

"He was behind a big mirror," Robert frowned, "The boss must have moved him."

I nodded, "I'm glad we found it, we can take him to the girls place tonight."

"He's a good magic mascot," Robert smiled, "we just need to make sure he doesn't go hiding from us again."

18

The Sleepover and the Witching Hour

Robert and I had showered, put our pyjamas on, and we'd put on our coats ready to go next door to the girls' flat. I had the skull and the Grimoire under my arm, and Robert had decided to bring over a jar of cookies he'd made recently. We knocked on the door together and waited for one of the girls to answer it.

"It's open!" Darling called out.

I opened the door for us, looking into the girls' apartment with wide eyes. The apartment looked very different to how I remembered it. As we stepped inside Robert and I could see why neither of the girls had been able to open the door. Lillith was sitting at their dining table, a large mortar and pestle in front of her, and she was chopping up some leaves which I could smell was rosemary from the door. Darling was shifting a trunk, which usually sat in the middle of the lounge room. She was moving it out the way so that we could all lay down on the floor tonight. Robert quickly put the cookies on the dining table to help Darling shift the trunk, while I sat down next to Lillith.

"What are you doing?" I asked.

"I'm preparing the ingredients so we can mix them together and make the protection circle," Lillith said, "Did the Grimoire say anything about when we're supposed to do this?" She asked.

"Actually, it did," I said, putting the Grimoire on the table and opening it to the page titled 'The Circle'. "It says we have to mark out the circle on the witching hour, but I don't know when that is."

"Oh, that's alright." Lillith smiled, "It's good you guys came over tonight, we're going to need to stay awake awhile."

"You know the witching hour?" I asked.

"The witching hour is between 3 and 4am," Lillith explained, "It used to be the only time of day or night that there wasn't a church mass going on. That's why it's called the witching hour, because it was the one-time witches could roam wherever they wanted without being spotted by churchgoers."

"That sounds really useful," I said, "Especially because we don't really want people to see us sprinkling this mixture around the shops."

"Both of them?" Darling asked.

"Yeah, if this protective circle actually works, we want you two to be safe too," I said.

"Oh, thanks Nav," Darling smiled.

I saw Lillith smile as she kept cutting up the rosemary. "So we can stay here and watch some movies, then at the witching hour I'll pass out bags of the mix and we can all make the circle around the shops." She added.

"What do you need me to do? I want to help prepare the spell," I said.

"Well, first you need to tell me what the Grimoire says about putting these ingredients together." Lillith said.

"Right, okay," I said, looking down at the Grimoire. I read a few of the sentences before I started to paraphrase for Lillith. "It says to make a fine white powder first, so I'm guessing that means the eggshells and salt."

Lillith poured in around half a bag of salt and almost all of the eggshells she had collected. As she started grinding them up with the pestle, she almost looked like she needed to use two hands. She kept mixing while I told her the rest of the instructions.

"After you've made a powder, you mix in the rosemary, and then make the whole lot black with the candle soot." I said.

"And how does it say we have to create the circle?" Lillith asked.

"We have to walk around at a steady pace, sprinkling the mixture as unbroken as possible." I said, scanning the page, "clockwise around the buildings, during the witching hour."

"Alright," Lillith nodded, "So I'll split the mix up between four bags, and then we can punch holes in the bags, so the mixture comes out continuously."

"That sounds like a good idea," I smiled.

We heard a knock at the door and Darling jumped towards it. "Oh, we ordered pizza, hope you don't mind." She said quickly.

Lillith shrugged, "We didn't really want to cook tonight, though we did pick some good movies to pass the time."

"That's alright," Robert beamed, "Spending time with you both is the most fun part."

We saw Darling pay the pizza man and close the door with her hip, before she set the pizzas down on the dining table.

"Alright, Hawaiian and a Cinque Formaggio, and garlic bread of course," She smiled at us.

"What's a Cinque Formaggio?" I asked.

"Italian," Robert hummed happily, "Must be good whatever it is."

"It means five cheeses," Lillith giggled.

"It's amazing," Darling smiled, "And we always get one."

"And we picked some good educational movies tonight," Lillith added. Darling passed us plates and we took a few pieces of pizza each. Darling and Robert had been setting up the lounge room while Lillith and I had been working together to make the protection powder.

"Educational?" I asked, scrunching my nose a little as I thought of the kinds of 'educational' movies they used to play for us at school.

"Well, witchcraft educational," Darling corrected, "We thought, seeing as that Nav was getting more comfortable with it all, he might learn something from a bit of fictional magic."

"Sounds fun," I said, a little hesitant to get too excited about it.

"Don't worry, nothing too serious," Darling said.

"I'm sure you'll be alright if we watch them until the end," Robert said, "You'll see things get fixed with magic as much as they can go wrong."

I nodded, sitting down between Robert and Lillith on the floor in the lounge room. "So what's first?" I asked.

"The first one is about a boy who goes into the magical world and has an adventure, its actually one of my favourites," Lillith said, "He goes looking for a star, but he ends up having to protect it from witches and princes and pirates too."

"Sounds fun," I nodded, "And if it's one of your favourites I'll trust you that it ends happily."

"Don't worry," Lillith said, leaning into me a little, "If there's a scary bit you can close your eyes."

"Oh, ha ha," I said, "I'm not that scared, I'll be fine."

"Alright, put it on Darling," Lillith grinned.

After about three movies Lillith looked at the clock and put the kettle on. The sound of the boiling water woke us all up a little. It was nearly time to put up the protective circle around the stores, and Lillith made sure we all had a cup of tea while she bagged up the mixture in four bags. At 10 to 3 in the morning, Lillith passed the bags of powder around, and lead us outside.

"Alright, so we need to walk this clockwise around the two buildings," She said, "Nav, do we need to say anything?"

"Only after the powder is scattered around," I said. "If we each take a specific spot to pour the powder, we'll be able to create the circle easier. Then we have to say 'Terra, Aqua, Aether, Ignis, hear our voices and protect this place.' After the circle has been made."

Lillith, Darling, and Robert all nodded, watching me closely.

"Where do we stand?" Darling asked.

"Nav and Lillith, you two stand at the back of the stores, I'll start at the front door of our flat," Robert said, "Once I get to Darling at the front of Grey and Hallward, then she can move around to Lillith, Lillith to Nav, and then Nav back to the front."

"Sounds like a plan," I smiled at Robert, happy to see him organising us. Lillith and I walked around the backs of our stores, Lillith behind Grey and Hallward, and I behind The Velvet Mansion. We waited quietly, making sure to keep looking over at each other to keep alert. It wasn't long before I could see Darling walking around the corner and Lillith started pouring out her bag of the mixture. I waited, I could hear my heart beating in my ears watching Lillith walk towards me with her bag of powder, leaving a trail behind her. When Lillith got to me she touched my shoulder.

"Tag, you're it," She smiled.

"Thanks," I smiled back, puncturing a hole in my bag with a pair of scissors she handed to me, and began walking away, past the back of the Velvet Mansion, then walking along the alleyway between my apartment and the black shop. I hadn't thought much about it since we'd moved in. The whole shop was black, even the bricks were made of a black clay I'd seen a few times around Ebonwick, but I'd never seen a whole building made of them. The windows were always closed, and you couldn't see through them because it looked like the windows were boarded up from the inside. I kept walking, looking back a little to check that the line of powder I was laying down was an unbroken line.

I could see Robert waiting for me at the corner of the shop, I guessed he was waiting for me so he could show me where the line started. I could feel my body buzzing, more than when we'd done the Binding Spell. I was actually excited about doing this magic spell. I was growing more confident the more I found out about magic and how useful it could be. I thought, a bit selfishly, how glad I was that I could read the Grimoire and the others couldn't. It felt more like the Grimoire wanted me to learn about the magic inside it, and that meant that I was learning about something I was *meant to*, rather than something that should be hidden and kept away from me. It wasn't that the others didn't deserve to know about magic, or that they weren't meant to help me figure things out, but it meant that I couldn't be left out of all of that knowledge, even if someone tried to keep me away from it.

As I got closer to Robert he began walking along the front of the shops, until he stopped in between them. I could see Lillith and Darling at the other end of the alley between the shops, waiting for me to finish the circle so that we could say the phrase together when it was completed. As I got close to the end of the powder line I looked up at Robert. He was smiling at me, a comfort just in time to stop me wondering whether this was a silly idea or that it wouldn't work. I finished the line of protection powder and looked through the alleyway to where Lillith and Darling were watching us.

Robert held a thumbs up to the girls and we began to say the phrase together.

"Terra, Aqua, Aether, Ignis, hear our voices and protect this place."

19

A New Kind of Nav

The next morning Robert and I woke up on Darling and Lillith's lounge room floor. We collapsed pretty quickly after the protection spell, and because we'd been awake so early in the morning it was already morning teatime before we woke up. I looked up with bleary eyes and saw Lillith in the kitchen making tea.

"Good morning," Lillith smiled.

"Morning," I rubbed my eyes a little. "Where's Darling?"

"She's downstairs," Lillith said. I watched her grab two cups of tea and she handed me one as I sat up.

"She's at work?" I asked, a little shocked.

"Darling has never really needed much sleep to keep going," Lillith said, "She might have a nap later though."

I nodded. I couldn't imagine Robert trying to function on only a few hours sleep. He always fell asleep when he needed to. He could sleep anywhere if he needed to. I once told him he could go to the Olympics for sleeping, but he gave it up when he realised he'd probably miss out on too much good food if he tried sleeping for that long. Besides, Ebonwick didn't participate in the Olympics anyway, even for something like marathon-sleeping. Robert had been stirring while we talked, and when he opened his eyes I could tell he still thought he was asleep.

"Morning," I said to him.

"Where's Darling?" He muttered, his eyes only half open.

"Wow, you two only share one brain in the morning huh?" Lillith giggled.

"Only sometimes," I said, still turned towards Robert. "She's working already Robert."

"Nooooo," Robert said.

"She is," I nodded, wanting to tease him a little, "We think she's an alien that doesn't need sleep."

"She runs on horror movies," Robert said, rubbing his eyes, "And probably coffee, and sometimes just pure riddles."

"Okay Robert," I smiled. I watched him close his eyes again and I turned to Lillith.

"Can he stay here for a bit longer?" I asked.

"Sure," she smiled, "Fancy coming with me to the Laundromat?"

"What for?" I asked. I was already going to come with her whatever the answer, but I was still curious.

"When Darling and I cleaned up yesterday I found a whole heap of dirty clothes," Lillith explained, rolling her eyes a little. "Plus I wouldn't mind some company if you're up for it."

"Oh, sure," I smiled, "I'll go get changed and see if we have any too."

"Sounds good," Lillith smiled. "Come through Grey and Hallward, that way I can tell Darling Robert's still here."

"Sure," I said. I was excited to go out with just Lillith again. After finishing my cup of tea I rinsed it in the sink and headed back over to the Velvet Mansion. I was glad that I'd brought my coat over last night, it covered up most of my pyjamas as I ran home again.

When I got back to Robert and my apartment, I bounced down the hallway so I could shower and grab new clothes to wear today. I decided I wanted to wear my black jeans and one of my collared stripey shirts, I saw them in my closet first and grabbed them. I stepped into the shower and made sure to wash my hair.

Once I got dressed I stood in front of the bathroom mirror and started to comb through my hair with my fingers. I'd towel-dried it and normally I would style it now, but something was stopping me. I ran my finger through my hair, shifting it from one side to the other. It was longer than I'd realised, and I hadn't paid so much attention to my hair for a while. I could see my natural brown hair growing out of my head, the roots were starting to show so I would have to colour them again soon. I didn't like that my hair wasn't naturally blue. It was a lot of work to maintain it, but I also hated how I looked when the brown started showing. The more brown my hair was, the more I looked like my brother Morgan.

Morgan and I did look extraordinarily similar, especially

when we were children. All of the baby pictures at my parents house were of Morgan, but no one who ever visited would have guessed there wasn't a picture of me on the walls. It was only when I went to high-school that we really started to look like two different people. I had a long face like our father, Morgan's was round like our mother and grandmother's. Our eyes and hair colour were the same though, and even though my face was different I still saw my little brother when I looked in the mirror at my brown hair. As soon as I was old enough to buy my own bleach and hair dye I turned it blue, and I had kept it up for years.

I decided today to change my hair and try and make myself feel better about the brown, so I parted my hair to the side and let it flop a little over my face. I combed the shorter side back and I didn't put any product in my hair, letting it stay fluffy. I wondered what Lillith would think, and I really hoped she would like it.

After my hair was finished, I tilted my head in front of the mirror, giving myself a little smile. I walked out into the lounge room and put my shoes on. I had my teal leather jacket hanging off my armchair and I grabbed that before I headed back out the door to go and meet Lillith.

She was waiting for me in Gray and Hallward, her shoulders were high and she looked like she was trying to shrink into her grey scarf. Lillith didn't seem to like the cold, which I thought was really sweet. She always seemed to have more layers on than the rest of us, even Robert. And I knew that Robert hated the cold weather. He used to bring hot water bottles to school under his shirt and it made him look like a massive warm bear.

She smiled as I opened the door of the art shop. I said hello to Darling before I instinctively picked up the large bag of laundry Lillith had by her feet.

"Ready?" I asked.

"You looked like you're dressed for a date," Lillith said.

"Well, I'm going out in public with you," I said, "we might have coffee, that's kind of a date." I smiled at her. She poked me, maybe she thought I was kidding. My cheeks felt a little warm, I felt like I should have been joking now.

"Is that alright?" I asked.

"Of course it is," Darling said before Lillith could talk, "It's really cute."

"Thanks Darling," I nodded to her.

"Yeah, come on then," Lillith smiled. She looped her arm around mine and led me out the shop.

We walked together around the corner before she spoke again.

"Do you think the protection spell worked?" She asked.

"Well, we didn't pass out this time," I said, "I feel like that's definitely a good sign. Though we did all collapse because we were so tired, so I'm not sure whether that counts as passing out or not."

"I wonder, how would we even test if it worked?" Lillith asked.

"Throw my little brother at it and see if he bursts into flames?" I asked.

Lillith let out a laugh that I had never heard from her before. It was sort of explosive, and I couldn't help laughing too. Explosive and contagious, nothing like her usual polite giggles I'd heard her make before. Even though this particular laugh sounded more like an elephant sneezing than anything else, I felt quite strongly that it was my favourite laugh Lillith had ever done. And my goodness I wanted to make her laugh like that again.

"Oh, sorry," she said as the laugh finished, covering her face a little with her mittened hand.

"That was amazing," I said. "Have you got a tuba in your coat?"

"Nav!" she sounded embarrassed. I tried to take it back, I didn't mean to upset her.

"It's alright," I said, pulling her closer with my arm that was looped with hers, "It was adorable actually. I must have said something really funny."

"It was just good timing I think," Lillith smiled.

I nodded, giving her a smirk.

"So, two spells down and one elemental personality test," Lillith said jokingly, "How do you feel about it all now?"

"I'm still working on it," I said truthfully, "I mean, it feels easier to think about it. It's a whole new world of information, and that's very exciting. I'm still wary of actually embracing it though."

"How do you mean?" She asked.

"Well, I don't feel like a witch yet," I said, trying to find the words, "I don't feel like my brain has fully accepted its real or not, or whether either of the spells we've done have actually worked."

"I feel like there's a 'but' there though?"

"But I think I've stopped arguing to myself that learning about magic is not for me." I said. "I think that, somehow, I've been told for years that magic isn't something I need or want to know. And I've started telling myself that if I really want to know, there's nothing that should stop me from learning it."

"That sounds like a Nav I'd hang out with more often," Lillith smiled.

"What are you saying?" I scoffed, "We see each other almost every day already."

"You know what I mean," Lillith giggled.

"I've only just started reading forbidden magical textbooks," I said, "I haven't gotten up to 'girl definitions' yet."

"True," Lillith said, "I guess I meant, that's a Nav I wouldn't mind as more than a friend."

"Like, a best friend?" I asked. I was hoping that she meant as a boyfriend, but I really needed her to say it.

"No way," She said, "Darling is my best friend, no way you're taking that position."

I smiled. We walked a few more steps, getting close to the doors of the Laundromat.

"I meant as a boyfriend," Lillith whispered, her voice so quiet I wasn't sure whether she wanted me to hear it or not.

I wasn't very subtle, I'd heard her and immediately tripped over my own feet, almost ripping the laundry bag as my shoe caught on it. She caught me before I fell on my knee. My hand ran through my hair and tugged a little at a strand of it.

"Yeah," I said, knowing I'd completely ruined the conversation anyway. "That sounds like it would be nice."

"Do you think?" Lillith smiled, looking at me like she wanted to laugh at how silly I looked. I did look silly, I couldn't argue about that.

"Yeah, I do," I tried to recover from my first reaction, "I would like to be your boyfriend."

Lillith's smile was so big I wondered if it was hurting her face. "And despite you're lack of charisma throughout this entire conversation, I'd like to be your girlfriend too."

For a moment as we entered the Laundromat I thought I was floating.

20

Silvan's News and the Fifth Element

"Nav?" Lillith asked, nudging me a little, "You haven't spoken in almost ten minutes."

I shook my head to focus. I couldn't really believe I had a girlfriend now. Lillith put some coins into the laundry machine and turned it on as I figured out how to talk again.

"Sorry," I stammered, realising I still hadn't spoken yet. "Must still be a bit tired."

"Oh," Lillith exclaimed, "Maybe we should go for that coffee now?" She asked.

"Yeah," I smiled, "That sounds good."

"Alright," Lillith smiled. She grabbed my hand and pulled me up from the chair I'd been sitting on.

As soon as we walked into Silvan's café I felt more relaxed. I could smell the rich coffee beans and hear the sound of the milk steamer. I saw Silvan turn and he beamed at us, flashing both his dimples while his eyes sparkled behind his round glasses.

"Hey you two," Silvan grinned. "What's brought you in here?"

"You don't need to ask that," Lillith smiled.

"True, true," Silvan said, "Coffees coming, they're on me today."

"Wow," I said, "What's the special occasion?"

"Apart from you two holding hands?" Silvan smirked at us, like he knew about the conversation we'd just had. Lillith and I made eye contact and we smiled at each other nervously.

"Actually, I'm kinda annoyed at my boss so this is the best way to get back at him."

"What happened?" I asked Silvan. I'd never seen Silvan look anything less than delighted before.

"He's closing down the café," Silvan sighed, "I finish up at the end of this week."

"Oh no," Lillith gasped, "Is there anything we can do?"

"You can't be serious," I said, my voice louder from the shock, "This place is always full of people, why would you close it down?"

"No, it's alright," Silvan shrugged, handing us our drinks, "I've got a good apartment with my friends, and it's just sped up my plans I've been saving up for."

"What plan?" I asked.

"I'm going to open my own coffee shop," Silvan smiled.

"Wow!" I said, "That sounds amazing, you'll have to tell us where it is."

Silvan laughed, "Of course, it feels good knowing I've got

so much support. Everyone I've spoken to today has said the same thing."

"Well, of course," I smiled, "You're the best barista in Ebonwick. I'm sure some of your customers would move town if you did."

Silvan waved a hand at me like I was joking. "I doubt they'd even miss me," he said.

"Come on Silvan," Lillith said, "I've been coming here for years, I've never seen anyone in a foul mood here."

"Thanks Lillith," he smiled, wiping down the counter around the coffee machine. "Besides, I think I've done enough travelling, I don't think I'd leave Ebonwick for a few more years."

"Where have you been?" I asked.

"I was born in New Orleans, actually," Silvan smiled. "My parents both spoke French so when my mum passed, I lived in France for a few years, worked on a lavender farm for a bit."

"That sounds so cool!" I said. "Why did you come to Ebonwick then, it sounds kind of boring in comparison."

Silvan chuckled. "Honestly, I think I stumbled upon Ebonwick when I needed to settle somewhere. I didn't have many friends until I came here, and the houses I lived in never felt like my own either. That changed when I came here. Ebonwick feels like home, more than anywhere else I've been."

I nodded, trying to process what he was saying. I'd never left Ebonwick, not even on a holiday. I couldn't really imagine what it felt like travelling somewhere else. I didn't even really know how to start planning to travel. It made sense why Silvan always seemed much wiser than his age though, if he'd travelled and experienced different places.

"What was it like working on a lavender farm?" Lillith asked him.

"The world becomes saturated with the colour and the smell," Silvan beamed, "I think it took about a year living in Ebonwick before I stopped smelling of lavender constantly. It was hard work, but it was so much fun."

Silvan stepped away to serve another customer for a moment, and I turned to Lillith.

"Do you think we should ask him about the elements?" I asked.

"Do you think he'd know about them?" Lillith asked.

"Well, maybe we could just ask whether he'd heard of something like it?" I said, "He seems to know a bit about magic, from what he's told Robert and I."

"Alright," Lillith nodded, watching Silvan walk back over to start making the customer's coffee. "Silvan, we wanted to ask you about something," she said.

"Anything," He said, nodding to show us he was listening.

"Actually, we were talking about the research we've been doing-," I started.

"I think Robert mentioned it to you before," Lillith added, helping me along.

"About magic," I kept going, feeling better that Lillith was beside me. There was no way I could have spoken about this to him without her. "We were reading about the four elements and trying to decide which one's the four of us had."

"Five elements," Silvan said in a tone that meant he was correcting us.

"Five?" I asked.

"Earth, air, fire, water," Silvan said, "and spirit."

Something at the back of my mind rang out like an alarm bell. That's what I'd been missing before. The first time I'd read the page about the elements in the Grimoire, it had mentioned spirit as well. But after that it had disappeared completely from the page.

"How did I forget!" I gasped. Lillith turned to me quickly and Silvan just seemed to smile a little more.

"Forget what?" Lillith asked.

"The Grimoire had spirit before, but it disappeared from the page after I read it the first time," I explained.

"It did?" Lillith's eyes grew wide, "Why would the Grimoire hide it from you? Isn't it important?"

"Yes, and no," Silvan interjected, "Spirit isn't something that is inherently present, it's something you create. It's an element that needs to be cultivated, not something you can just bottle up and use later."

"So how do we know when we've created the spirit element?" I asked, "Surely we'd need to know it was present to make the spells work."

"Well, you know how people say they can sense ghosts even though there's nothing there? Or how you can feel the energy in a room of people at a party?" Silvan asked.

"Not really," I shrugged.

"Yeah," Lillith said. We'd spoken at the same time, our answers kind of melting together.

Silvan chuckled, "You know that feeling you get when you just know someone's going to like something even if they've never actually talked about it before?"

"Oh, yeah," I smiled. That had happened a few times when I'd bought Robert birthday presents.

"That's the kind of thing that spirit is," Silvan said, "It's the 'knowing but not knowing' kind of instinct that we have."

"So, how's that make it one of the big magical elements?" I asked, "If it doesn't have a physical presence?"

"Well, it's the element most closely linked to the magic itself," Silvan explained, "When you create magic with the four physical elements, spirit is what pushes the spell into the real world. You can have all the ingredients and fancy words in the world, but without the energy of the spirit, specifically the spirit of the witch themselves, you don't have a spell."

"So, we all have spirit?" Lillith asked. This was one of the few times I'd ever seen her look so uncertain of her own knowledge.

"We do, though it's not something that is just 'switched on' all the time, that's why it's so difficult to define." Silvan replied.

"Does that mean that maybe the grimoire hid it because we weren't ready to read about it? Because it's difficult to define?" I asked. I didn't know how a book could change its own pages like that, but there must have been a reason I had read the word 'spirit' on the elements page before it had disappeared.

Silvan nodded purposefully, finished pouring a coffee and handed it over to the customer. When he turned back to us there was a glint in his grey eyes that suggested a kind of mischief I didn't expect. "Now you know about the elements, which one did you figure each of you were?" he asked.

"Nav is water, Robert is earth, Darling is air," Lillith said.

"But Lillith doesn't fit into any," I added, "That's why I thought we should ask you."

"Have you considered that Lillith moves between the elements because you guys are fixed?" Silvan asked.

"What do you mean fixed?" I asked.

"Well, you're saying that you three are very strongly your element," Silvan said, "You aren't born with a strong elemental pull, you grow into it based on how you're raised and how you grow. Lillith might have grown up learning to move between the elements for different reasons, and that's why she doesn't fit into any one elemental personality."

"So it's okay I'm not fire?" Lillith asked.

"Of course," Silvan smiled, "You react to things as they come, using different skills depending on the other people around you. That's a very difficult thing to learn as well as maintain."

"That's an interesting point," Lillith said, "What do you think?"

"I think Silvan's right, though I don't understand why the Grimoire didn't talk about the spirit." I said, "I can't believe I didn't remember reading it in the title before."

"Might be something that your Grimoire wanted you learn after the initial four," Silvan suggested, "so that you manage the four first before using excess amounts of your own energy to make magic happen."

"Alright," I nodded, wondering whether I should go through the Grimoire again to look for anything on 'the spirit'. I turned to Lillith, "Actually, we probably have to start getting back to the shops."

"Thank you for the advice, Silvan," Lillith said as we went to leave the café. "It was really helpful."

"Thank you!" I called out too, "And let us know when your café is open!"

Silvan waved goodbye to us and we walked next door to the Laundromat to collect Lillith and Darling's laundry. Once we had bagged them up again, we started walking back towards our shops. Lillith leaned close to me while we walked, and I wondered what she was thinking.

On the walk home Lillith looked ahead and started walking slower. I slowed down so I didn't walk away from her and looked towards the shops that were now very close to us. We slowed to a stop and I saw an old man walking purposefully towards Gray and Hallward.

"That's Mr. Peters," Lillith said.

"That grumpy old man?" I asked.

Lillith nodded, "He never buys anything, just comes in to complain how lazy young people are these days."

I nodded slowly, watching the man walk sharply towards Gray and Hallward, before stopping a few steps away from the front door. He looked around, before starting to walk quickly in the opposite direction, away from the shop.

"What happened?" I said.

"He didn't get a phone call," Lillith said. She started walking again and I caught up with her. She was looking at the ground. "He just stopped."

"Wait, the protection circle we did," I said, "Do you think it classed Mr. Peters as an evil that couldn't cross it?"

"Well, I wouldn't say he's evil," Lillith said, "Though he does make Darling and I exhausted every time he comes into the shop."

"That might be enough," I said, "Magic seems to be very personal."

We came to the spot in front of the shop that Mr. Peters had stopped at, and we looked at the floor. There was no line of powder anymore, the rain had washed it out, but we could see a faint crack running through the pavement. I didn't know if it had been there before, but if it was the protective circle, we'd just seen it in action.

21

Testing the Circle

We walked into Gray and Hallward and saw that Robert and Darling were sitting together at the counter talking. Robert still had his pyjamas on, but it seemed that he'd fixed his hair and he looked awake talking to Darling. Lillith walked past me with the bag of laundry, taking it to the back of the shop just in case a customer came in.

"Well, we know the protection circle works," I said after checking the shop to make sure we were alone.

Darling and Robert made the same face of surprise as they looked up at me.

"How do you know?" Robert asked.

"When we walked back here we saw Mr. Peters try to walk in, but he turned around at the circle like he'd forgotten something." I explained.

"I didn't even see him walking up," Darling said. "Are you sure it was the circle?"

Lillith walked back in the shop then, hearing Darling's question. "He was walking with such a purpose towards the shop, and nothing happened until he got to the circle. It was as if he'd gotten a phone call and needed to rush somewhere, but he never got anything out of his pocket."

"It was like when you go to buy groceries, and you stop and wonder if you should buy cookies, but then you see someone from school and you need to disappear quickly." I said.

Robert nodded at that, getting up from his seat. "Well, it's good we know that it works," he said.

I nodded back at him. "Oh yeah, and we found out that Silvan's coffee shop is closing."

"Oh no!" Darling exclaimed.

"What's going to happen to him?" Robert asked.

"He said he was going to open his own café," Lillith smiled, "He's going to let us know when it's open."

"That's brilliant!" Robert said, "We'll have to keep an eye out for that. Though I do think that I need to get out of my pyjamas now," he said.

"Yeah, we should get back to The Velvet Mansion," I said. I looked over at Lillith and realised she was mirroring my smile.

I steered Robert a little so we could leave Gray and Hallward and go back home. "Bye Darling! Bye Lillith!" We called out.

"Bye!" The girls chorused back as we stepped out into the street and started walking back to The Velvet Mansion.

We walked a couple of paces away from Gray and Hallward when I got too excited to tell Robert what had happened earlier.

"Hey Robert?" I said, my steps getting a little bouncier the closer we got to The Velvet Mansion.

"Hello Nav," Robert replied.

"Guess what."

"Walruses have magnificent moustaches, but they could just be seals in disguise?" Robert asked.

"No, though I am suspicious of walruses now," I said.

"Then what my good pal?" Robert said jokingly.

"I have a girlfriend now." I said.

"NO!" Robert yelled with excitement. He smacked me across the shoulder and I stumbled. "NO!"

"Calm down!" I said, rubbing my shoulder, "That hurt." I was actually a little worried that the girls would hear Robert because he was so loud.

"Sorry," Robert said, "I'm just excited. How did that happen?"

"We were talking about how much more confident I've gotten from learning more about magic, and how we've done two spells now, and Lillith mentioned that I was becoming a different kind of Nav than when we first moved in."

"That's true," Robert said, "I haven't seen you lose all focus thinking about Morgan or your parents for a while."

I nodded, "I didn't quite realise it until we were talking about it, but then Lillith said that she wouldn't mind dating someone like the new kind of me."

"Is that a pick-up line?" Robert asked.

I shrugged, "I don't know, but I asked if that meant she wanted to be my girlfriend, and then suddenly, I had a girlfriend!" I said.

We had gotten to the door of our flat, and I unlocked the

door so Robert and I could go in. I was smiling so hard my cheeks were getting sore, but I didn't want to stop either. I watched Robert processing what I'd said, he was smiling too.

"I'm very happy for you Nav," Robert grinned.

"Thanks Robert," I said. I watched him start walking down the hallway to his room so he could get dressed. "Tea?" I asked.

"Yes please," Robert called. I could tell he'd left his bedroom door open so he could keep talking to me as he got dressed. As long as I didn't walk past his room it was fine. I started boiling the kettle when I heard him call out to me again.

"Did you change your hair?" Robert asked. I knew he was asking so I wasn't too embarrassed. He'd seen me with the same hairstyle for years.

"Yeah, I did," I replied to him, "Trying to let it grow out a little more before I kill the roots."

"It looks alright," Robert said, I could tell he was trying to sound supportive. "Hey Nav?" He said after a moment.

"Yeah?" I asked, making us both a cup of tea.

"Do you think, with the protection circle," Robert said, "Do you think we could use it on Jules?"

"How do you mean?" I frowned. The spoon made a louder clink against my tea cup than it usually did.

"Well, the whole point of it was that it keeps out things that could harm us," Robert said. His voice got louder as he walked back through the hallway to the kitchen. "Neither of us really know if Jules was telling the truth the other day, so maybe we could let the protective circle decide?"

"You think if we invited him over, we could see if he could step through the circle to the shop or not?" I asked.

Robert shrugged a little. "Well, if it turns out he really does want our help, then the circle would let him in. If he's just trying to get something out of us, he'd be turned away like you saw with Mr. Peters."

I thought about it for a moment. Robert had a good point, the protective circle was like a magical bully detector, in theory. Robert definitely had more trust in people than I did, and the fact that he was still wary of Jules coming back to the shop said a lot. He also sounded like he'd thought a lot about this idea, testing Jules with the protective circle we'd just put around the shops.

"It sounds like a pretty good idea," I said slowly, "But if you invite Jules over here, I don't want to be in the shop."

Robert nodded with understanding. He knew that I took it pretty hard when we stopped talking to Jules, though I'd never completely explained to him what had happened. He hadn't actually been there the last time I'd spoken to Jules, though I'd told him about some of it afterwards. Most of my explanation was anger-filled teenage ranting at the time though, so I wasn't sure how much of it was the truth anymore.

"What about if you could watch, see if he crosses the circle, and then come talk to him if you wanted?" Robert asked. "I'm sure if we explained it to the girls they'd let you watch from their flat. Then you wouldn't have to talk to him if you didn't want to, whatever the circle says."

I nodded, thinking it over. "Okay Robert," I said, "If Jules wants to come over, just let me know when he does."

"Alright," Robert said. I saw him get out his phone and start moving his thumbs over to send a message to Jules. "Do you think Darling would be my girlfriend?" He asked, his voice quiet.

"I think she would," I said, "The amount of giggling she does when she's around you, I'd say she was close to asking you herself."

"Really?" He asked.

"Yeah!" I said. I smirked a little, planning to tease him a little. "I mean, it's not hard getting a girlfriend if you're charming like me."

"You mean if you stumble enough, you eventually get the right question out," Robert teased back.

22

Jules Comes to Visit

Robert had gotten a reply from Jules later that day, and they arranged for Jules to visit in a few days. The morning of Jules' visit I had woken up very early with a nervous stomach, and I was soon over in Lillith and Darling's flat, looking out the window for Jules. Lillith sat down next to me and handed me a cup of tea in one of her wonky mugs. You could tell which mugs were Lillith's in their flat, because all of hers were handmade ones, and they were oddly shaped and had interesting glazing on them. Darling's mugs were all movie inspired, and most of them seemed to be special editions that she'd bought online.

"Do you really think Jules might be evil?" Lillith asked.

"What kind of evil?" I asked her back.

"The kind that a magical circle can stop?" She tried.

"Maybe," I said. "I don't think he's proper villainous evil, I just think he can't be trusted."

"Okay," Lillith said. I looked over at her for moment and she gave me a little smile.

"Besides, Mr. Peters wasn't evil, just draining," I added, "And the circle worked on him."

"True," Lillith nodded, "And what if it lets him in?"

"Then, I guess," I thought about it, and I wasn't sure if I wanted to believe it yet. "I guess that means that he does actually want to fix what he did."

"What did he even do?" Lillith asked.

I shrugged, "He used to be our friend, he lived across the street from me. But we went to high school and he ended up with all these new friends, and he forgot about us."

"Well, lots of people drift apart," Lillith tried.

"It was like he became a completely different person," I said, sounding a little annoyed, "All he cared about was expensive clothes and trends and what was popular. He was not the Jules that we were friends with."

"So he got popular, made new friends," Lillith said, "What then?"

"He stopped talking to us, he even acted like he didn't know me at all," I said, "I tried to confront him about it and he just claimed I was lying."

"How do you mean?"

"Well," I started, I haven't even told Robert the whole story, and I didn't know if I would. Robert still had some good memories of Jules, and I didn't really want to ruin those memories like mine had been. "I found his group outside a bar one day, I don't even remember why I was out by myself. But I tried talking to him, asking him about ditching Robert and I. I asked him why he was being such a jerk to us."

"What did he say?" Lillith asked, her eyebrows furrowed.

"He didn't say anything," I said, "Just looked at me blankly, frowning at me like he'd been bothered by a noise but his eyes didn't focus. Like he wasn't sure if he could see me or not. I remember wanting to push him when he tried to turn around without responding, and the next thing I knew I was on the floor with a busted lip."

"He hit you?" Lillith asked.

"I don't know," I said honestly, "It's weird, I don't remember the feeling of pushing him, and I never saw him move, but something had definitely hurt me. I didn't talk to him again after that, and I told Robert to stay away from him."

"I'm surprised Robert didn't go after him to avenge you," Lillith said, her voice light. She made me smile a little, and I decided to joke with her to clear the air.

"Robert wasn't the burly figure he is today," I smiled a little, "He used to bruise so easily that even if he'd just fallen out of bed he looked like he'd gotten into a fist fight."

"Really?" Lillith asked.

"Oh yeah," I said, "he didn't get much sleep in high school, and he was quite fragile for a bit. Sometimes I almost wasn't sure if he was still in the room, I thought he might fade away into thin air at any moment."

"This is the same Robert Bard we're talking about?" She asked.

"Oh yeah," I nodded, "After we stopped worrying about Jules he got a lot better."

"I'm glad he did," Lillith said, "I can't imagine you without Robert."

"Neither can I," I said, "If I lost him, I don't know what I would become."

Lillith nodded. We sat for a little while, looking out onto the street that ran past the front of both the shops. Rosemary Route was a quiet street most of the time, the majority of walking people gathered at The Last Drop and most didn't go further unless they were specifically looking for The Velvet Mansion or Gray and Hallward. Even the little tea shop next to The Last Drop was a quiet place, and I'd only seen 3 old ladies go in there since Robert and I had moved in.

"What's he look like?" Lillith said,

"Tall, kind of stretched," I said, absent-minded, "with curly blonde hair, and the fashion sense of a university professor."

"I think I see him," Lillith nodded, pointing at the pavement just outside of The Last Drop crowd.

I looked over to where she was pointing and saw him starting to walk down the pavement across the street from the shops. Even from this distance I could see he'd made an effort to look comfortable and friendly, like he used to do before we went to highschool. He was wearing a light pair of jeans and a light grey knitted jumper. A white collar poked out the top of the jumper and I could see him looking down to stop the rain going in his eyes.

"That's him," I nodded.

"I think I've seen him before," Lillith said.

"When?" I asked. I was a little surprised, given that Robert and I had only seen him recently. We had successfully not seen Jules for a few years after high-school, I didn't know why Lillith would have seen him.

"A year or so ago," Lillith frowned, "I saw him talking to those two girls, the ones who we've seen around taking photos of people."

"The ones who work in the cake shop that had no name?"

"Yeah," she nodded. "I actually thought he was the person who ran the underground modelling agency for a while."

"Really?" I asked, "Do you think that's where he's been?"

"I don't know," Lillith said, "He doesn't look the same as I last saw him, he's far... less."

"What do you mean?" I asked, "He's thinner?"

"No," she shook her head, trying to think, "No he seems less, his overall personality is smaller than before. Last time I saw him I felt this strong feeling that he was a very powerful dangerous man. Now, it seems like he's lost all of that. Almost like he's a blank slate again."

I had been listening closer to her words, and when she said the words 'blank slate' I remembered something he said earlier, when he'd spoken to Robert and I.

"Jules said he didn't remember much from the past 6 years, that there was a blank spot in his memory." I said.

"You've had that before, haven't you?" Lillith asked, "You told us about how you didn't remember anything strongly until you met Robert in school."

I nodded, "Do you think it could be the same thing?"

"I honestly don't know," Lillith said, "But it sounds like Jules is trying to find out."

"He's coming to the circle," I said, leaning forward to watch him. He looked around; his pace slow. I wondered if he was nervous about talking to Robert, or whether he was trying to think his way through the meeting before it started. He came to the line where I knew we had laid the circle down a few nights before. He didn't stop, like Mr. Peters had, he kept walking over the line and towards The Velvet Mansion. I could hear my heart through my ears for a moment, realising that whatever Jules had done didn't matter, the magic we had done trusted him.

"He walked through," Lillith said, her voice quiet.

"He did," I sat back, letting a long breath out. I didn't know if I was relieved or shocked, but I was definitely a bit stunned by the outcome.

"Nav," Lillith said, squeezing my hand a little. I looked over at her and saw a gentle look in her eyes.

"I think you should go and talk to Jules," she said.

"Yeah, actually," I said, a little louder than I expected. I breathed deeply in and out again to steady myself. My thoughts were happening so fast that I couldn't actually focus on any of them. "Yeah, I think I should talk to him."

"The magic said he wasn't dangerous, and if the memory blanks are connected?" Lillith added.

"Then we can probably help each other to figure it out," I nodded.

Lillith nodded. She got up and took our empty coffee mugs to the kitchen. I stood up and followed her, shaking out my legs as I reminded myself how to walk.

"Thank you, Lillith," I smiled.

"That's what girlfriends do," She smiled back.

I stepped closer to her and kissed her cheek before I got too nervous and turned away. It was quick and light, but my heart was pounding anyway and I felt the hair on my arms tingling like I'd been electrocuted. Her smile grew wider and I bounced towards the door with my coat.

"Dinner at ours?" I asked, "We can tell you and Darling about what happened with Jules."

"Sounds good," Lillith grinned, "We haven't had gossip that good in ages."

23

Mixed Up Memories

I strode quickly towards The Velvet Mansion, hearing my footsteps sharp on the pavement. I was going to talk to Jules, to try and figure out what happened all those years ago. I wondered if he had remembered anything since we'd last seen him, or whether he wanted to talk to Robert about something else entirely. When I got to the stairs that led down to The Velvet Mansion I stopped, wondering whether I actually wanted to go in. Out of everyone who knew me younger than the age of 18, Jules Bambroke was the last one I wanted to talk to now. I took a deep breath in and decided that, he might be the last one I wanted to talk to, but I was going to make the effort to hear him out. He might have some new information about his memory loss after all, and I still wanted to know why he changed so much in high school.

I walked down the steps and opened the door of The Velvet Mansion, seeing Robert and Jules on the chairs near the back of the store. My back was tense, I could feel the muscles in it tightening. Robert looked up at me with a huge grin on his face. The corner of my mouth lifted slightly and Robert nodded. The nod wouldn't have meant much to anyone else, but I knew it spoke better than Robert could. It was a nod that said 'I'm proud of you' and the look in his eyes was one of such excitement that I was going to give Jules a chance.

"Hey Nav," Robert said, "There's an extra chair here." He pointed beside him to another large armchair which he must have moved this morning when I left.

I smiled properly this time, feeling a wave of relief. Robert knew I was coming, of course he did. I walked towards them, glancing over at Jules. I wasn't as good at reading Jules anymore, but his features seemed to move differently today. They were far softer than when I'd confronted him at school, though that might have just been my memory. Jules smiled when I sat down and I made a small shrug at him. He jumped a little, like he'd been extremely rude for a moment.

"Did you want tea? Robert made some earlier," he said to me.

"No thank you," I said, as cheerfully as I could, "I had some with Lillith before I came over." I had said it without thinking, but as soon as her name had come out of my mouth Jules leaned forward. As he got closer I could see a glint in his eyes, it may have been excitement but I couldn't be sure. I was already feeling overwhelmed by the situation, I wasn't sure that any of my impressions of Jules would be right today.

"Robert's been telling me about your friends," Jules smiled, "Tell me about Lillith?"

"Well, actually, Lillith is my girlfriend," I said, my heart speeding up a little.

"Oh Nav," Jules gasped, his eyes wide, "That's awesome!"

"Yeah," I smiled a little. I'd forgotten how explosive Jules got when he was excited. "Yeah, she's amazing."

"And her bookshelf?" Jules asked.

"Full of fairy tales and other worlds," I said. It was something that we'd once talked about, many years ago. Jules was the one who'd taught me the best way to look into someone's personality was by looking at their bookshelf.

Jules looked over at Robert expectantly. Robert nodded, I think confirming that I was telling the truth. Jules was grinning from ear to ear.

"Oh Nav, she sounds perfect," he said, "I always knew you'd find someone to teach you about that stuff."

"What stuff?" I asked. I wondered if Jules was actually happy for me, or whether he was jealous I had a girlfriend.

"Magic and fairies and things," Jules smiled, though as soon as he had his eyes grew wide.

"What's wrong?" Robert asked.

Jules was still for a moment before he shook his head, "Nothing, sorry, I thought I was remembering something."

"About magic?" I asked. I watched as Jules eyebrows frowned and he opened his mouth in shock as I said the word 'magic'. I knew it would surprise him but I was also secretly enjoying that I had more knowledge than Jules. He always seemed to know the answers to everything when we were kids, and I trusted his every word, but it was nice to be the one who had the knowledge now, at least a little bit.

Jules tilted his head to one side. "I never thought that Nav Green would be asking about magic."

"I've changed a lot over the years," I said, "Most significantly in the past few months we've been living here."

Jules nodded slowly, "Robert's been catching me up on some things, though I'm still confused about why we're not friends anymore."

I clenched my fists. Then I realised and I sat back in the armchair. I didn't want to get too angry with him, I needed information. I wanted to know, more than anything, why Jules had suddenly found us again now. He hadn't made an effort to get in touch for years, so something must have happened recently to change his mind.

"You really don't remember?" I asked. The air in the space above us seemed to go still, and Jules fiddled with his shirt sleeves.

"Actually, no," Jules said, pausing to try and find the words, "Sometimes I look at something and I feel a strong emotion, but I don't have a memory attached to it."

"Like what?" Robert asked.

"Well, when I looked at my mother, I could feel this weird, feeling," Jules said, "it was like, a wanting, and then disgust, and then nothing, like everything went quiet. But they weren't my emotions either, or I wasn't actually feeling them. I was remembering feelings that I no longer had, but were still attached to her."

"What did you mean, a wanting?" I asked.

"Like the feeling you used to get when you wanted this one thing for Christmas, or when you go out and see something that you know is far too expensive. That feeling that you wished someone would just buy you everything you want and there's no consequences afterwards."

I was nodding suddenly, "You seemed to be getting increasingly expensive things," I said, "I don't know how your mum managed it." His mum doted on him, it was just the two of them in their house afterall, but the Jules I knew didn't want for very many possessions. Even as a small child he'd been a minimalist, and all his presents seemed to be things he could share with others; cooking books and utensils, or board games mostly, and he rarely wanted something just for himself. That was, until he changed in high school.

"I was so happy to see her again," Jules said, looking down at his feet, "You don't know how shocked she was when she opened the door. She told me that she hadn't seen me in three years. Three years." He was speaking softly, almost like he was stuck, and his expression was dropping quickly. His shoulders moved forward and for a moment I wondered if he was going to cry. "What happened to me?" he asked, his voice a whisper. It seemed like he was scolding himself more than asking us. Robert and I looked at each other, unsure what to do. Luckily, Robert spoke first.

"Jules," Robert said, his tone much gentler than if I had tried to calm Jules down. "We could help you figure this out, the memory loss. We don't know all of it but know more or less how things started."

"I know what you're going through," I said suddenly, surprised I was even going to tell Jules this, "I have some memory loss too, maybe we can work through it together?" I wondered if my memory loss and Jules' were caused by the same thing, and maybe if it was linked to something magical I could fix my own memories while we helped Jules.

"You do?" Jules asked, "When?"

"From before I met you and Robert, and some gaps just after. Mine's more occasional, but there's still very decent gaps in it."

"Why didn't you tell me?" Jules asked.

"It wasn't something I wanted you to worry about," I said. A nervous laugh escaped my lips as I realised, "I knew you'd try and be a detective and figure everything out, and I was worried my mum wouldn't let me hang out with you anymore."

"I remember once she was furious that I'd tried to find her family recipe book," Jules said, "I'd only wanted to make some pancakes. Do you remember? She caught me in the very back of the kitchen cupboard and looked like she was going to throw me in the oven." He laughed a little when he finished talking.

"I never understood why," I said, "She never could cook anything, but she never let anyone try either."

Robert shook his head, "Out of every threat your mum said to me, she never thought to use her cooking against me."

We all laughed at that. It was lucky in some ways that my mum never wanted Robert to stay for dinner, because he made every effort not to eat her cooking. Just smelling the oil sizzling in the kitchen would have Robert racing out the house and calling his mum to come pick him up.

After a pause Jules looked at me, his eyes filling with

something like begging. "So, will you help me try and patch my memory back together? Please Nav," he said.

I let myself look deep into his eyes, searching for anything that might suggest he was lying. But I found nothing. All I could see in his dark blue eyes was despair, and a plea for help. I still didn't know if I could trust Jules or not though. I wondered whether, if we helped him with his memories, whether he'd turn back into the person he was in high school, or whether he'd stay like he was now. Robert had sat quietly watching me as I thought, and when I leaned back in my chair again, I could see him starting to smile.

"Alright Jules," I nodded, thinking that maybe I'd just have to risk it and see what kind of person Jules was now. "If you're serious about this, we'll help you."

"Thank you," Jules sighed gratefully, jumping up to his feet. He shuffled forward and then back again. It was a move I hadn't seen in ages. He had been close to bouncing over and giving me a hug, but he'd suddenly thought better of it. "Thank you both," he looked at Robert and they exchanged a nod too. When he had sat back down in his chair I'd had an idea.

"What do you think we should do first?" Robert asked.

"We should start at the end, I think," I said, "Robert and I know about the beginning, at school, but we don't know how you came looking for us, it might give us some clues to go on."

"That's a brilliant idea," Robert smiled at me. "Go on Jules, start from the end and be slow about it," Robert grinned at him.

Jules thought for a moment, like the memory was hard to think about. Then, he started to talk.

24

Beginning At the End

I was too hot, that was the first thing I noticed. I opened my eyes slightly, though my head was still fuzzy from sleep and I couldn't quite process what I was looking at yet. I wiggled my foot and felt a slippery material around me. My arm moved out from the covers so I could sit up, the first time I tried it slipped and I looked down. The sheets were red, made of satin. Why was I sleeping on satin bedsheets? I sat up and got dizzy for a moment. It was strange, it felt like I was floating above my body, it seemed too far away.

I looked around the room and my heart started racing. This wasn't my bedroom. I could see some clothes folded neatly on the edge of the bed and I grabbed them quickly. I shook out the black leather pants, they looked far too big for me but I tried them on anyway. My eyes widened as I put them on, they were a perfect fit. More than perfect, it was like they were tailored to me. I seemed to be towering above my feet. Maybe I had finally had a growth spurt?

I couldn't wait to show Nav and Robert how tall I was. I did have to figure out where I was first though.

"I'm not in Cashton Grove anymore," I said to myself, smiling a little. I took the shirt that had been folded with the pants and held it out. I scrunched my nose up a bit looking at it. It was one of those silken blouses like a pirate would wear, but if pirates had a designer brand. There was no way I was wearing that. I looked around, looking for what might have been a wardrobe. Something about the place did look almost familiar, like I wasn't particularly surprised to see what was there.

I found the wardrobe, at first I thought it had been a black mirror. I pressed the doors gently and they swung open, making a whooshing sound as they did. My eyes widened more when I saw how big the wardrobe was inside. There were so many racks of clothes I didn't know where to start, but then I realised they were in colour order, and I gravitated straight for the light blue colours. I shifted through a dozen shirts before I found a nice one. It was a collared shirt, buttons down the front, blue pinstripes on it. I put it on quickly and this fit me perfectly too. It even had a secret pocket on the inside, a detail I had always wanted in a nice shirt. I didn't know who's place this was, but they sure had style.

I looked for a pair of sensible shoes but found a lot of heels instead. Right at the back of the wardrobe I found a single pair of pointed business shoes with glittery white laces tied in them. I put these on and wondered if I had brought my satchel with me to this place. I couldn't find it anywhere, so I went towards the door of the room. That was the first time I was looking at the whole room at once. I stopped in my tracks when I saw the picture above the bed for the first time.

It was a portrait, painted like a Botticelli painting from the Renaissance. A figure in a small roman toga, lounging on a hill surrounded by ladies I could only describe as being 'ethereal'. They looked more like angels than people, bright shimmering wings and pointed ears. I frowned a little as I noticed something about the man in the centre of the party. The pale skin, the blonde curly hair shining in the oil-painted sunlight, a single birthmark on his shoulder that crawled over to his chest slightly. I looked down at my feet again, noticing again how far up I felt, how tall I was. I looked back at the painting and frowned, then tilted my head. I held my hands up in front of my face, and that's when I saw how long and slim my fingers had grown. The backs of my hands were much, much older than fifteen. I was older than fifteen. I had grown up, and that was me in the portrait. This was my room. How could this be me?

A knock on the other side of the door made me jump away, watching as someone opened the door. Her hair was bright red and curly, hanging over her shoulders and down her back. She was surprised that I was on the other side of the door, but she smiled and presented a large tray she had walked in with.

"Breakfast as usual," she smiled.

"Uh, sure," I said, watching her walk over to the bed and set the tray down. "Sorry, I must have slept heavy, who are you?" I asked.

She was taken aback; I didn't really blame her. "Hope," she said after a moment, "I'm guessing you're going out to recruit new models then?"

"I am?" I asked.

She giggled, "Well you only dress that normal when you're going 'to the surface'," she made air-quotes with her hands.

"Normal?" I laughed nervously, "I thought the leather pants were already a bit much."

She frowned a little like she hadn't expected that from me. She stayed quiet, though I could tell she wanted to question me too.

"Since I'm going to the surface, can you just remind me where I am?" I asked, trying not to sound too panicked by this whole situation. She frowned even more, I could tell I was pushing my luck with that question.

"You're the same place you always are," she scoffed, "You really must have hit the bed hard last night."

"I must have," I said. I wondered for a moment whether I could just leave and get a taxi home without knowing where I was right now. It seemed like the easiest way to get out of here without asking Hope any more questions. "Hope, uh, my wallet?" I asked.

She walked around to the bedside table, the same side I'd been sleeping on. She picked up a large black wallet from the table and tossed it to me.

"Thank you," I said, pocketing the wallet.

I watched her eyes grow wider and she suddenly made to pick up the tray. "Okay then, I'll take this back if you're not hungry."

"Thank you, I'm not," I said. My stomach rumbled quietly to object, but I really just wanted her to leave. She nodded, frowning as she took the tray and left. I was so confused I had to sit down on the bed again, trying to think over the conversation. Her reactions to me seemed to tell me a lot more than what she actually said.

I felt an itching in my hands, I needed to get out of there and out into the open. I opened the door and came into a large room full of lights and mirrors. There was a strong scent of floral perfume and something else that might have just been the smoke pooling around the floor. I couldn't do it, I turned around and went straight back into the bedroom that might have been mine. I shut the door quickly and leaned my back against it, petrified. I had an idea and took out the wallet Hope had thrown at me.

When I opened the wallet I was confronted by pictures of myself. There was a variety of shiny cards filling the slots of the wallet and each one had my name stamped boldly across the top. Some were cards for restaurants, some for banks, some for clothes shops, all of them maxed out to the platinum level. In the other compartments of the wallet I could see wads of cash threatening to spill out at any moment. I frowned and picked out what might have been a driver's license. I didn't remember driving at all, but I had a license to if I wanted. The photo looked less like a means of identification and more like a headshot for a magazine. I raised an eyebrow as I looked at my birthdate printed on the license. It wasn't my birthday. Instead of being dated on Valentine's day, which was my birthday, it was dated for sometime in June. Something had happened in June that I couldn't remember, though I knew it was important. Whatever it had been it didn't really matter to me right now, all I knew was I had enough money to get myself home.

I opened the door, trying not to let the large room overwhelm me again. I looked quickly and found the door on the other side of the room which I assumed was the way out. I ran through door after door, it felt like I was in a maze trying to find a way out. I didn't walk up any steps though I could feel in the air somehow that I was getting closer to the street level. Finally, I walked through a door and squinted in the light, gasping at the noise of the busy street and the people suddenly walking past me. I had escaped, from what I didn't know, but I was so relieved to get out of the dark rooms that I didn't think to look around where I had come up to.

25

What Happened To Us?

"What happened then?" Robert asked, looking at Jules intently.

"Nothing," Jules said, looking between Robert and I like he was still a bit lost in his memories. He shook his head and spoke again, "I hailed a taxi, gave them my mum's address, and left. I don't even really remember the drive; I was too anxious just to get back to something I recognised."

"So, you don't remember anything before then?" I asked. I was suspicious of his story, it almost seemed too easy for him to have left that place without anyone stopping him. It was even a little strange to me that he didn't remember where he'd come out to the surface in town, there wasn't many places in Ebonwick that might have access to a 'secret underground'. There were shops under street-level, plenty of them like The Velvet Mansion, but to have something underneath those places? I didn't know how it was possible.

"Nothing," Jules shook his head. "I've woken up a few times from a nightmare, but I never remember anything about it."

"Nightmares," I mused. That was something I knew well, disturbing dreams that made me talk in my sleep. Robert had recorded some when we were teenagers, but it freaked me out too much to know what I'd said, and I'd told him to stop.

"And, after you met your mum?" I asked him.

"I spent a week with her, asking what had happened to me and getting used to my age." Jules said, he had a smile for a moment and shrugged his shoulders, "It's still a bit weird knowing I'm an adult when the last memories I have are from when I was 15."

Robert and I nodded, knowing how weird that would be for us too. Jules spoke again, a little hesitant now.

"After a few days my mum explained that I hadn't spoken to you two for years, and that she didn't know why. I wanted to know what had happened between us, so I asked Nav's parents where you guys were. I'm sorry I had to track you down the way I did, I just didn't know what else to do."

"So you do admit that you tracked us down?" I asked, frowning at him.

"I didn't do anything illegally," Jules insisted, "I just asked your parents Nav, and I've tried to be as transparent as possible telling you both all of this. I know I must have made some pretty big mistakes as soon as I saw you guys outside the coffee shop, all I want to do now is find out what happened. And I want to see if I can fix some of it," his voice quietened the more he spoke.

Robert leaned forward, giving Jules a comforting smile. "Well, I think we'll try and help get your memories back."

Jules looked over at me, asking me with his eyes whether I agreed with Robert about helping him.

After a moment I nodded. I knew how much losing your memories could affect a person, and I still wondered if helping Jules might help me sort out some of my own memories.

"We'll do our best to help you sort some things out," I said. And if you go back to your old habits, I thought to myself, losing you again won't change anything for us this time.

Jules's face lit up and he looked like he wanted to get up and hug me. I leaned back slightly and he understood why. We weren't 'back to normal' yet, it would still take a while for me to trust him again. I wasn't really offering him a best friend yet; I was only offering him help with his memories.

Jules sat back, his feet shuffling a little. He tugged at his jumper sleeves again and I knew he was about to ask a serious question.

"Can I ask, what stopped us being friends?"

Robert opened his mouth to talk before turning to me too. "Well, Nav knows more than I do," Robert looked almost guilty for not being able to explain what had happened. Jules turned to me slowly and raised his eyebrows, waiting for me to tell him.

"Well, people change a bit when they get to high school, don't they?" I said, trying to make my voice sound light. Jules raised an eyebrow at me before shaking his head a little.

"Changed?" he asked, wanting me to continue.

"We were put in separate classes," I said, "Robert and I in one, you in the other. I guess, when you were in class you started making new friends? We weren't there so you didn't get immediately labelled as 'friend of the weirdos', so I guess it was easier for you to talk to other people." I started.

"I wouldn't have cared if I was," Jules said. I looked up and saw his face was flushed. If he was angry at that I didn't know how he was going to take the next bit. "I remember being put in separate classes, talking to new people, that's before my memory stops." He said.

"Well, that's how it started," I told him, trying to sound calm. I did wonder if he just wanted another argument, but when he went quiet again I continued. "You were still hanging out with us at lunch, but you disappeared more and more, you were becoming popular and we didn't really want any of that-,"

"Not that we didn't want to be bullied either," Robert added, "just that you were hanging out with some weird people."

"How weird?" Jules asked.

"Well, in a way that isn't a compliment," Robert replied. He tried to think of how to describe them. "They were, almost too perfect."

"Nobody's perfect," Jules shook his head.

"No, they were actually perfect," I said, remembering what Robert was talking about. "All of them got perfect marks, they were all the 'star' of each and every after-school activity, they never got into trouble for anything no matter how many rules they broke, they couldn't do wrong by anyone."

"They didn't even suffer any of the teenage dramas either," Robert said, starting to count on his fingers. "No spots, no spills, no outfit disasters, no trips, no scratches."

"They were impervious to imperfections," I nodded, "And

they had this weird ability to get all the attention they wanted, and then disappear as soon as something went wrong."

We all sat in silence for a moment. I put my hand behind my head and tugged at my hair a little. Jules hands moved around themselves, like he wanted to fiddle with rings that he could feel on his fingers but weren't actually there.

"So, anyway, we started seeing less of you. I think you just liked the idea you didn't get bullied anymore." Robert said.

After another moment Jules nodded. He took a deep breath and looked up at us. "I could relax, I didn't have to be on edge the whole time waiting for someone to come up to us."

"We saw you on holidays, but less and less in public," I added.

"I knew you didn't like them," Jules said, "They didn't like you much either Nav, though I can't remember why."

I shrugged, though I thought it was kind of amusing that Jules's friends didn't like me. I'd always tried to be somewhat invisible at school, so for someone to actively dislike me they'd have had to be paying attention for a while. Of course, bullies were everywhere even in Ebonwick, but normally they didn't have an active reason to dislike me like Jules's friends did.

"Even among weirdos," I smiled, "I'm the weirdest of them all."

"Well, you and me both," Robert smiled at me, "No Nav without a Robert."

"So, when did we stop hanging out completely?" Jules asked.

Robert and Jules looked at me. I knew Robert probably wouldn't remember, because he was already working his early bakery job. He didn't have much time to realise when things changed. I remembered though, and I alone had to tell the next part of the story. It was hard for me to remember it all so I could recount it to Jules, but I did want to see how he reacted to what I was about to say.

"Well, your friends were all going on this camping trip, to the woods behind the art college."

"The Shadow Wilds?" Jules asked.

I nodded. "You invited me along because Robert was busy working, but my mother wouldn't let me go because some of the woods were 'outside town'. I tried to argue that I'd be with you and a whole group of people, but for whatever reason she grounded me so I couldn't go."

"Of course she grounded you," Robert said, "even with Jules she couldn't guarantee you wouldn't hear ghost stories." He wiggled his fingers in front of him as if 'ghost stories' was synonymous with real and evil magic. I could see him smirking a bit, knowing that we were thinking the same thing. She'd be horrified to know that, even with her constant groundings throughout my childhood, I'd still discovered magic as soon as I moved out of her house.

"Then what?" Jules asked, "You didn't go on the camping trip, but I did, and then I came back different?"

"Not right away," I explained.

"What do you mean?"

"Well, the rest of your group came back a week before you did." I said, "Your mum came looking for you at my house, she told my mother your friends had told her you weren't ready to come home yet."

"But I did come back?" Jules pressed.

I nodded. "I saw you walking into your house, trailing mud and covered in leaves and twigs from the forest."

"Twigs?" Jules whispered to himself.

I thought the memory was finished but something felt like I should think on the image a little longer. Something that I hadn't registered before that might have been useful to tell Jules. Then it hit me, something I'd never realised before though I'd seen Jules with it multiple times since.

"And you were carrying a thin wooden stick, like a wand but shorter. I remember seeing it later, you'd turned it into a quill and always had it tucked behind your ear."

"A quill?" Jules asked, frowning with confusion rather than anger.

I nodded. "I didn't really remember that part until now, but I don't think I saw you without it until you showed up again looking for us."

Jules sat back in his chair. His eyes were wide but they weren't focused on anything. His gaze was somewhere in the depths of the antiques around us, and his thoughts weren't in the store at all. Robert and I looked at each other, not really sure what to say next.

"So," Jules said, his voice quiet. His eyes were still off in the distance as he spoke, "That was it? I came back and I was, changed?"

I took a moment to think of what to say, and Jules turned to look at me. I took another deep breath in and told Jules the truth.

"You weren't yourself at all," I said, "You forgot Robert and I existed. You didn't change Jules; you came back a different person with the same face."

26

Help In Turn For Secrecy

"Wait, do you guys think someone replaced me?" Jules asked suddenly.

"I would have thought it was a logical possibility," I started, "But you wouldn't have woken up in that room if you'd been replaced." I wasn't sure how something could replace Jules and look so exactly like him either, let alone use his voice and remember pieces of his life.

"Yeah, you'd have woken up in the Shadow Wilds," Robert agreed with me, "So you couldn't have been replaced."

"My personality completely changed though," Jules pointed out, "and I don't remember anything of that time, so I couldn't have just changed on my own."

"Maybe this is one of those things," Robert started, "you know, when people say they were 'possessed'?"

"Possessed?" I asked. I frowned at yet another gap in my knowledge, and I knew already it must be something connected to magic that my parents would have swept out the house.

"Like, something other than them is controlling their body," Robert explained.

"What?"

"Most people used to blame it on demons," Jules added, "though mostly people think it used to be a person's mental health that just made it *look* like they were possessed."

"Right," I nodded, "Old age medicine couldn't explain what they couldn't see, therefore it was evil?"

Robert nodded, "Evil or magic, one of the two."

A shiver went down my spine at the mention of magic. "Do you think that you could have been possessed?" I really hoped that wasn't the case. With books that moved on their own and magic powder that protected magic, I wasn't sure I was ready for something 'possessing' people as well.

"I've no idea," Jules said, "though I don't think demons exist, do they?"

"I'd rather it wasn't demons I think," I said, "though that wouldn't explain how you all-of-a-sudden woke up and didn't remember anything."

"Wouldn't it?" Jules asked.

"Well, it might," Robert said, "depends I guess, say if Jules was possessed, whether whatever had control on him left willingly or not."

"How do you mean?" I asked. If something that evil had control of Jules, I didn't think there was any way to get rid of it. But if that was the case, Jules wouldn't be sitting in our antiques store now asking us where 6 years of his life had gone.

"Well," Robert started, "I don't know much about people being possessed, but don't you think that if it left Jules voluntarily, it wouldn't have let him wake up in it's bedroom? It would have put him somewhere inconspicuous, and probably given him some false memories."

"Why would I need fake memories?" Jules asked.

"Well, think about what you're doing now," I said, catching on to what Robert was saying, "If you were possessed, then whatever it was wouldn't want you asking questions or going to look for it, would it? It would want you out of the way, because it technically stole 6 years of your life."

Jules started to nod as I spoke. "You're right," he said, his voice soft, "So whatever it was didn't expect me to wake up like I did, otherwise I wouldn't be with you guys trying to figure it out."

"We could ask Darling about it later," Robert said, looking at me, "I'm sure one of her horror stories might have something similar in it."

I nodded at him, "She might be able to help us come up with more ideas."

"So," Jules said, pausing to look at both of us. "So, you'll help me then?"

I thought for a moment. What Jules had told us wasn't what I expected, but it also made me very curious. I was still unsure whether Jules and my memory loss was the same thing, though it did seem to have the same symptoms so far. Now I could read the Grimoire too, I might even be able to find something that could help us.

I thought hard, looking at Jules closely in his eyes. I was looking for a hint of mischief, something that might have told me whether this was joke or not. "Sure, we'll help you," I said warily. "But I want you to promise you won't talk to your mum or my parents about what we're doing."

"Why's that?" Jules asked.

Robert cut in, "We've just been talking about lost memories, possible demonic possession, and magic," he said, giving Jules a look, "Why do you think?"

"Right," Jules nodded slowly, "I understand."

"So, we have a deal?" I asked.

"Our help in exchange for secrecy," Robert clarified.

"Deal," Jules nodded.

Robert and I nodded too. I wasn't sure what we could say next, but we suddenly heard an alarm go off. Jules jumped and fumbled into his pocket, getting out his phone.

"Sorry, I uh, I have to go," he said, looking down at his phone.

"Sure," I said, standing up from my chair as Jules did the same.

"Something wrong?" Robert asked.

"No, no," Jules said, "I just have a job I need to get to."

"Job?" I asked.

"Well yeah," Jules said, "You know what I said about my wallet being full of money?"

"Yeah, with lots of expensive cards in it," I nodded.

"Well, I decided to exchange the credit from all the shops, and I'm gifting the money to one of the charity shops in Centre Square." He explained. "I don't remember what my job was before, but I've found out I've got far too much money than I need, so I'm trying to fix that."

"That's-,"

"Sounds like the old Jules to me," Robert smiled at him.

"Yeah," I nodded, "That's a good thing you're doing."

"I told you I'm trying to make amends," Jules gave me a small smile, "In more ways than one. Though I am glad you'll help me try and figure out my memories."

"We'll try," I said, watching him closely. I did wonder whether we'd made the right decision, but Jules was already walking towards the door.

"Thanks for letting me come and talk with you," Jules said, looking back as we followed him to the door.

"We'll see you soon Jules," Robert waved him out.

"See you," Jules waved before walking out the door of The Velvet Mansion and up the stairs to the street.

27

Did We Break the Circle?

We watched as Jules walked out of The Velvet Mansion, up the stairs to the street, and turn to walk across the road. After he was out of sight, Robert sat back down in the armchair he'd been occupying while we talked to Jules.

"I'm glad you came to talk to him," Robert said, looking over at me.

After a moment I nodded, "Me too, it was, well, it was interesting at least."

"Do you think he was telling the truth?"

"Well, the protection circle said he was alright." I shrugged, "That means he shouldn't be any harm to the magic we've been doing. I don't think so anyway."

"I guess so," Robert gave me a little smile, "he did seem pretty upset that he's missing so many memories."

"Well, if you turned into a monster for years, forgot what

you did, then had to face all of those consequences at once, you'd feel pretty miserable too." I said.

"True," Robert nodded, "though it seemed like he was really sorry about your falling out in high school."

I sighed, "Yeah, I think he was too."

It was a little hard to admit it, but Jules did seem like he was trying. I didn't quite know if this was a good thing or not yet, but it did seem like Jules was good enough to come back into our lives for now. At least the protection circle thought so. A silence settled on us for a moment before Robert spoke, his tone hesitant.

"Do you think that getting Jules memories back will help him?" he asked.

"I don't know," I replied, "Lillith suggested that Jules' memory loss might be a similar thing to my own, from when I was very little. She thought that maybe helping Jules might help me remember some things too."

"I guess it depends how bad some of his memories are," Robert added, "if they're good, he'll be able to keep going with what he was doing, only nicer. If they're bad, he might need our help to fix a few things."

I shrugged at him, "Even if we can't help Jules remember all of it, maybe just helping him start over will be enough."

Robert nodded though he didn't look like he agreed with my words completely. He stood up then from his chair and grabbed his coat off the back of it. I tilted my head at him to ask what he was doing.

"Going to go tell Darling and Lillith what happened," He smiled, wiggling his arms into his coat. "I'm sure they're curious about what we talked to Jules about."

"True," I smiled, "They might have some ideas about the missing memories too, how we might be able to get them back?" I grabbed my own coat from the coat stand next to the door of The Velvet Mansion, and put it on while Robert made his way back towards me.

"Right, to Gray and Hallward!" He said, pointing into the air purposefully.

"To Gray and Hallward!" I copied him, stepping out of The Velvet Mansion and waiting for him to follow me outside.

He locked the door behind us, and when we were both ready we took the little steps up to the main street level. I walked close to where we'd laid the protection circle, feeling excited to tell Lillith about our talk with Jules. Robert's grey coat billowed out behind him as the wind picked it up, and we were walking in the lightest rain we'd seen since we moved into The Velvet Mansion.

As we got to the door of Gray and Hallward we slowed down. Someone was walking out of Gray and Hallward, their long brown coat wrapped tightly around their neck like they were preparing to walk through a blizzard. The thin white hair on his head was combed perfectly, and he looked like a very well-to-do retired man with old ideals about the world. The old man stepped out of the shop in front of us, his pointy shoes clicking on the pavement, and as he looked up we stopped dead on the pavement.

"Ah! Good afternoon gentlemen," Mr. Peters said, placing his hat on his head and shuffling quickly back across the road.

"Nav?" Robert said quietly as we watched the old man shuffling quickly down the street, "That was the man that the protection circle stopped before, wasn't it?"

"Yes Robert," I said as my heart started to race and the hairs on my arms stood up, "Yes it was."

About The Author

Shelby Rhodina was born and raised in Rockhampton, Australia, and always dreamed of becoming a published author. She started writing her first original series The Ebonwick Chronicles in high school, and at 20 years old self-published her first book, The Velvet Mansion and the Discovery of Magic in 2021. Shelby studied a Bachelor's in Visual Art, before continuing onto a Master's Degree in creative writing to further her dream career. In January 2022, Shelby received the Australia Day Cultural Award in Rockhampton for her efforts writing, publishing, and distributing her book in Rockhampton and Yeppoon. At the end of 2022, Shelby published her second novel, The Laundromat and the Four Elements, a sequel to her first novel. When she isn't writing Shelby is making art, and her sculptures and drawings both inspire and influence her writing.

To find out more about the world of Ebonwick, go to: www.shelbyrhodina.com

Or follow Shelby's Instagram: @shelbydraw01